MW00929395

ABSOLUTELY, POSITIVELY
NATTY

ALSO BY LISA GREENWALD

The Friendship List Series

The TBH Series

ABSOLUTELY, POSITIVELY NATTY

LISA GREENWALD

KATHERINE TEGEN BOOKS
An Imprint of HarperCollins Publishers

Katherine Tegen Books is an imprint of HarperCollins Publishers.

Absolutely, Positively Natty
Copyright © 2023 by Lisa Greenwald
All rights reserved. Printed in the United States of America.
No part of this book may be used or reproduced in any manner
whatsoever without written permission except in the case of
brief quotations embodied in critical articles and reviews. For
information address HarperCollins Children's Books, a division of
HarperCollins Publishers, 195 Broadway, New York, NY 10007.
www.harpercollinschildrens.com

ISBN 978-0-06-306272-6

Typography by Molly Fehr
23 24 25 26 27 LBC 5 4 3 2 1

First Edition

For my miraculous niece and nephew, Barbara Hattie and Joseph Allyn: I wish you both a lifetime of only wonderful but also the ability to feel your feelings and be supported by people if and when things get tough

1

THERE'S A QUOTE I HEARD once about trusting the magic of beginnings, and I can't remember how it goes exactly, but that probably doesn't matter.

All I know is, right here, right now, I'm trusting the magic of *this* beginning. That's what matters.

"Well, I should be getting back to Grandma and Grandpa's. Unpacking and everything," my dad says finally, after he fills out a million forms. "Have a good day, Natty. I know this is tough."

"What do you mean? It's not tough at all," I answer, smiling.

He tilts his head. "Well, I'm sorry we arrived so late last night, and it's all pretty last minute and everything."

I shuffle my feet on the floor a little. "No way! Sometimes arriving early to stuff gives you more time to be nervous. Now I'm just kinda thrown into it, like jumping right into a cold pool. You get used to the water much quicker that way."

"Okay, well, um, I guess that's one way to look at it." He hesitates. "I'll see you after school, okay?"

"Okay, Dad. Love you."

"Love you, too, Natty. Take it easy."

I stand there in the hallway and watch him walk away, and I look around: beige lockers, canary-yellow linoleum tile, a row of bulletin boards next to the office, like where people would hang flyers and stuff. Except they're mostly empty. There's one lunch menu from last June, half hanging off, and a very faded map of Pennsylvania.

I can't believe no one decorated them for the first day of school, when everything should be fresh and perfect and beautiful.

I wander around a little more, hoping to find a good place to sit and go over my schedule.

After a few minutes, I find the gym and peek in and then I see a slightly cracked-at-the-top glass door leading to the track.

When I get outside, I tilt my head to the sky and feel the glorious morning sun on my cheeks. I sit down on the bleachers and take my phone out of my pocket, and at that exact second I get a text from Gracie. We're so in sync it's like we read each other's minds, even from different states!

Gracie: Natty! Good luck on your first day. You'll be amazing as always. Everyone's gonna want to be your friend!

Gracie: Also is it weird you're starting middle school twice?

Me: Hiiiii. lol to starting middle school twice. Yeah, it's technically called Junior High here, idk. Just 7th & 8th grades.

Me: Got to school sooooo early to do paperwork. Sitting outside on the bleachers rn getting tan. Good luck on the first day of 7th grade! Can't believe I'm not there. And ILY sooooooooooooo much.

Gracie: CANNOT BELIEVE you're not here either! Miss you beyond.

Me: FaceTime later?

Gracie: kk

I look up from my phone and see that there's a kid running around the track. He doesn't look like a runner—he's wearing Birkenstocks with backstraps and baggy, khaki cargo pants and a tie-dyed T-shirt that says, "Waffle House."

He finishes a lap and looks up at me and then he does a little salute thing. So I do a salute thing back even though at that point he's not looking at me anymore.

Halfway through his next lap, he stops and puts his hands on his knees, bends over, and shakes his head like he's not sure he'll survive this. Then he starts running again and screams, "Gah! This is torture!"

"You're doing great," I yell back, and then cover my mouth immediately. Why on earth did I just say that? I don't know this kid. I don't know anyone here.

"What?" he yells back at me, almost completing the lap.

I laugh. "I said you're doing great!"

"It's my last day of this!" He screams, still running. "Hallelujah!"

I think he needs more support. Clearly, he's not into exercise, so I'm not sure why he's doing this, early in the morning before the school year's even started. This whole scene is very confusing.

I stand up and shout, "You're doing great! Keep running! You can do this!"

He pauses when he finishes the lap and makes it to my spot on the bleachers. "Did Sheila in the main office tell you to come out and cheer for me?"

"Huh?" I laugh. "What do you mean?"

He squints. "Who are you and what are you doing out here?"

"Oh, um, I got to school early to do all the new-student paperwork, so I figured I'd come soak in some sun before the day started." I pause. "I'm Natty."

"Okay, well, Natty, since you're new, here's my PSA: never skip gym. I failed last year for skipping too many times, and instead of having some kind of summer-school program like a NORMAL SCHOOL WOULD"—he yells the last part—"they told me to come run laps every day. EVERY SINGLE DAY OF THE SUMMER. That's it. Just run laps and then someone from the main office, usually Sheila, comes to check that I'm doing it, and signs my sheet. But hallelujah, today's my last day!"

"Well, yay for finishing it!" I say. "You're a pretty fast runner."

"Thanks, but it doesn't matter, 'cuz after today I'm never planning to run again!" He sings that last part, like in an over-the-top opera voice, side-smiles, and gets back to the laps.

I lean against the bleachers and tilt my head toward the sky again. So far I'd say this morning has been a win—sitting in the sun, cheering someone on—that's putting good energy out into the universe, no doubt about it.

I take my phone out of my backpack to make sure it's switched to silent before I walk into school and that's exactly when it rings.

"Hello," I say quietly since I'm not sure I'm supposed to be taking a call on school property.

"Nat. Hi. Did I catch you in time before school?"

"Hi, Mom! Yes! I'm about to go in and start the day. How are you?"

"Good, getting along." She sounds tired. "I made a plan

with Mally. Remember my old college roommate?"

"Yup! Of course! How is she?" I sit back and wave to Running Kid as he hobbles off the track. He doesn't see me.

"Doing well. . . ."

There's silence on the phone and I wait for my mom to ask me questions—how the ride to Grandma and Grandpa's was last night, if anything's new in Miller Creek, if that little diner down by the creek with the amazing banana walnut pancakes is still open. But nope. Nothing. Silence.

So I jump in. "It's really great here, Mom. Like honestly, so different from just coming on Thanksgiving and in the summer, like twice a year; just living here is different. Y'know? I mean, it's only been one night, but yeah, I can totally tell how different it is; it's really great."

"Mmm-hmm. That's wonderful, Natty-love. Anyway, just wanted to wish you good luck on your first day, and um, I hope you always know I'm here for you."

"Yup. I do." I swallow back the teeny, tiny lump in my throat. "Love you, Mom."

"Love you, too, Natty-girl."

I hang up then. I feel a little sniffly after she calls me Natty-girl because she's the only one who calls me that and now she's not here to say it and on the phone it just feels so different.

But I push away that feeling, and I don't dwell on it, because eventually she'll be here. Eventually she'll find

her way back to us. To me and to Dad, and we'll
fresh and it'll be a whole new thing, better than it's ever
been. I'm going to make sure of it.

It's like the quote I saw tacked to the wall above the
register at the place where Mom and I used to get our
nails done together.

"Sometimes good things fall apart so better things can
fall together."

I think it was Marilyn Monroe who said it, and she was
totally right.

2

RIGHT NOW, WALKING INTO MY first day here, I have all the amped-up, first-day, excited feelings I had when I started middle school the first time on Long Island. And all the "I wonders," too. I wonder what my teachers will be like. I wonder who my friends will be. I wonder where I'll sit for lunch and what books I'll check out of the library. I wonder if there will be gum stuck underneath my desk and if the bathrooms will be gross and if kids will call out without raising their hands. I wonder if my locker door will get stuck and if I'll accidentally get shoved in the hallway.

I look down at my schedule and see that Advisory is my first period of the day. Perfect. Such a good way to ease into things. It's like a class but not really a class.

At the top of the paper, the lady in the main office wrote, "Locker 46 in the B wing. Make a left out of main office and keep walking until you see it."

But now I'm at the gym and I have zero clue how to find the B wing. I look around the hallway filling up with students now. It's like I'm frozen right here on this square of linoleum, and I might never make it to my locker.

I walk three steps to try and see if the sign above the bathroom indicates what wing I'm in, but nope.

All it says is "Quiet in the Hall," but the paint on the Ls is mostly peeling off, so it looks like "Quiet in the Ha," which makes me laugh for a second, until I remember I'm really lost and have no idea where to go.

I feel like I should have been paired up with a buddy or something. That's what they used to do for the new kids who moved to Willets.

"Are you lost? You look very lost," someone says, and it takes me a moment to figure out where the voice is coming from. Then she comes closer to me and glances over my shoulder, at the paper in my hands.

"Oh, your locker is near mine. Come with me," she says flatly. "Welcome to Miller Bleak. . . . You're, like, the first new kid we've had in four years."

"Really?" That feels surprising. In Willets, we got a few new kids a year. "Well, thanks so much for guiding me!"

I take a deep breath and exhale and realize that the

positive energy I just put out into the universe by cheering for Birkenstock Runner Kid totally paid off! Now someone is helping me!

"I really appreciate this," I add. "I'm Natty, by the way."

She nods. "Cool."

"What's your name?" I ask, trying to fill the silence.

"I hate my name. Let's just do the 'hey you' approach, okay?"

"Okay." I stop myself from saying that I'm not the biggest fan of my name either and that's why I'm so loyal to my nickname.

We walk quietly the rest of the way, and when we get to the lockers, she says, "Well, here we are."

"Thank you again."

"Please stop thanking me. Seriously." She cracks her knuckles and throws a few notebooks into her locker with a thud. "I never finished unpacking my bag from last year. Oops."

"Your backpack is really cute. I like the stripes," I say.

"It's old. I wanted a new one but oh well." She looks at the floor and picks at the nail polish on her thumbnail.

"So, um, do you have any advice for me?" I ask, wishing I knew when the bell would ring. "I mean, I guess you're new to this building, too, since the school starts in seventh grade, so the whole grade is new, so, yeah. . . ."

She looks over at me. "Do you know how to read a room? That's where I'd start."

I nod. I get it. My stomach twists up after she says that, like I need to run away right this minute, and calm myself down. But I am not going to do that. Things are fine. Things are good. She doesn't want to talk right now, and that's okay. I can read a room. I can totally read a room. Or in this case, a hallway.

I will read a room. I will read every room. I will be the best reader of rooms in the history of reading rooms.

I'm ready for it.

Finally, the bell rings and the girl walks on ahead of me.

I look down at my sheet to see what classroom Advisory is in, and I figure out, based on the A before A53, that it's in the A wing and I know that's where the gym is.

I'm doing great so far!

Unfortunately, I walk into class, and there's Read a Room girl again and I still don't know her name.

She's the only one there so far, so I sit down and wait for others to get here, and I don't say hi or anything. I just sort of smile in her direction and hopefully she knows I'm open to talking if she wants to. Hopefully she can see that I'm reading the room.

It's silent in the classroom except for the extremely loud ticking of the black-and-white clock above the door. I don't know how anyone takes tests in here and is able to stay focused with that tick-tick-tick-tick.

I take out my notebook and doodle and try to stay occupied until more people get here.

"Do you really mean that?"

I look up, confused at first, but then I realize Read a Room girl is actually talking to me again.

"Mean what?" My voice catches in my throat.

"Your patch. On your backpack."

I look down at it and then back at her.

"'Good vibes only,'" she says, like she thinks I'm confused and doesn't know why I'm not getting what she's saying. "Do you really believe that?"

I hesitate a second because I don't want to say the wrong thing. This girl is actually talking to me, and maybe this is a good sign. I can't ruin it so soon after it's started.

"Why aren't you answering me?" she juts her head out in my direction.

"I do believe it," I say finally. "I believe in good vibes."

She throws her head back, laughing. "But *only* good vibes?"

I pick at some rough skin on my pinkie. "I mean, kind of, yeah. What's the point of bad vibes? I think positivity is kind of contagious. If we have a good attitude everything can actually *be* good—actually it can be better than good; it can be *great!*"

"Wow. Okay. Long explanation." She shakes her head at me like I'm from another planet, and she doesn't say anything else. She still hasn't told me her name, which feels really, really weird, but when I peek over to her desk

I see that her green spiral notebook has MACK at the top in lopsided bubble letters.

I guess that's her name. Mack. I'm not sure why she hates it so much. It sounds cute to me.

A minute later, a teacher walks in, and then a bunch of students follow behind, like they were all together somewhere and finally decided to make an appearance.

"Students, welcome," she says. "I'm Ms. Lamlot and this is Advisory, where you'll start the day, every day. I'm here to be a listening ear, a voice of reason, a mediator, a sounding board, a guiding light." She pauses and clasps her hands together against her chest. "Welcome back to the building. I hope you remember everything from the tour a few weeks ago." She pauses again. "Namaste, everyone. Namaste."

I look around the class to see if this is a normal thing that happens in Miller Creek, but everyone is just sort of sitting there, staring at this person. I like her, though. She reminds me of my mom with her yoga vibes, and I feel like we'll really get each other.

Ms. Lamlot sits down in her wheelie chair that wobbles more than glides. "So, first of all, let's all welcome our new classmate." She looks down at a piece of paper on her desk. "Natanya Blaken." She smiles. "Stand up, Natanya."

My face feels like a radiator that's been on too long, but I smile and wave, and then I say, "Oh, actually call me

Natty. I don't really go by Natanya."

"I've never heard *that* name before," a girl in the row behind me sneers to her friend. Then a few boys in the back stand up and do a sort of over-the-top clapping thing and then Ms. Lamlot quiets them down.

"Blaken . . . sounds familiar to me." She pauses. "Do you have an older sibling, maybe?"

"Oh, um, no." I shake my head and sit down. "Maybe you're thinking of my dad. Keith Blaken? He grew up here."

"Dude! She's not that old. She couldn't have been your dad's teacher!" Some kid shouts from the back, and a bunch of other kids cackle, and again Ms. Lamlot needs to quiet them down.

"Oh, yes! Keith Blaken! Of course! We were in the same graduating class. Good guy!"

I smile, feeling like this connection is everything, somehow. Like yeah, I'm in this new school, and the kids seem a little prickly and some of the paint is peeling off and the door leading out to the track was half broken, but this teacher actually knows my dad! It's like coming home in a way. This is huge.

"Okay, students," Ms. Lamlot says in a soft voice, her hands clutched against her chest. "For this first day, please take out a piece of paper and write your name and your contact info and one phrase that could sum you up."

"Huh?" a boy in the second row calls out. "What does that mean?"

"A phrase that can sum you up, doofus," the boy next to him says. "Like 'Just keep swimming.'"

Then the other boy smacks him on the side of the head. "You're saying that 'cuz you're literally a swimmer."

"Students, students," Ms. Lamlot says. "This is not how we behave. Deep breaths. Everyone. Three deep breaths in and out."

The rest of the period sort of goes on like that and I put down my favorite saying: "The grass is greener where you water it," and then the bell rings and it's time to go.

That "phrase that sums you up" thing was really easy for me.

I'm grateful for that. It's another good sign for the year.

3

IT TURNS OUT MACK IS in every single one of my classes, but somehow I make it through the whole day without really interacting with her much. We're in ninth period study hall, but we don't have anything to do because we haven't gotten homework yet. The whole class is loud and hyper and kids are screaming and throwing balls of paper at each other. And the teacher just sits there at his desk at the front of the room, typing on his laptop like he doesn't care.

"Students, eventually you'll be glad you have this time each day to complete homework," he says, not looking up. "For now, please just talk quietly. No need to scream. No need to scream."

"As I was saying." Mack turns to me and starts talking, like our conversation from the morning is still ongoing.

I'm realizing she doesn't have many (or any) friends. She hasn't talked to a single person all day. Maybe she did at lunch, but I didn't go to the cafeteria. Once I realized we were allowed to take our lunches to the library, I decided that was a better plan for the first day. Sometimes it's good just to jump right into stuff, and other times it's good to ease in. Knowing the difference is the important part.

"Yeah?" I turn to her.

"As I was saying, why does it need to be good vibes only?" She taps her pencil eraser against the side of her head.

"'Cuz what's the point in focusing on negative stuff?"

"Because it's real. Life isn't, like, all sunshine and rainbows and puppies." She turns her whole body to face me and pulls her knees up to her chin so her dirty white Converse are now on the chair. "Where do you even come from? Is this some sort of experiment? Are you even a real human girl?"

I laugh. "Well, yes, I am human. Thanks for checking, though. And ummm. It's kind of a common phrase. I didn't make it up. You've never heard the phrase 'good vibes only' before?"

"I have. And it's dumb. But you seem to, like, 'be' the phrase." She uses air quotes for the last part. "You're, like, way too smiley."

I laugh for a second, even though I think this girl may hate me, but that's okay. There's a lot of room for improvement here. "I don't really know what you're talking about, Mack."

"Whoa, way to know my name even though I never told you."

I laugh again; I can't seem to help it. "We've been together this whole day. Of course I know your name. They took attendance in every single class. Plus it's at the top of all of your notebooks."

"Wow, you're creepy."

Finally, she turns away from me and starts doodling on her paper, but her doodles are really, really good. A few minutes later, she looks up and says, "Anyway, my new mission is to prove to you that bad vibes are okay. It's better just to acknowledge when things suck."

I shrug. "Sure. Fine. Go for it. It's always good to have a mission."

Mack shakes her head at me. "We've said like three words to each other and you're pretty insufferable, so I don't know why I am still talking to you, but sometimes I do dumb stuff, Natty or whatever your name is."

I smile. "Yup. You got it right. It's Natty."

The bell rings, finally, and everyone leaves the class, and Mr. Study Hall teacher still doesn't look up from his laptop.

So far Miller Creek Junior High is pretty much the opposite of my old school. In Willets, we had pizza fundraisers every Wednesday after school, and a Fall Fair with a Ninja Wall set up in the parking lot, and sometimes the cafeteria would even have California rolls on the salad bar.

I head toward the bus line, but then I realize that I don't want to get on it. My grandparents' house isn't so far from here. I can walk. I want to clear my head and shake off Mack's weird attitude.

That kind of negativity is just pointless and dumb. There's no reason ever to focus on the things that stink when there's so much good stuff to think about.

"Natty! Hi! You scared me," Grandma says as I walk into the kitchen, the screen door slamming closed behind me.

"Oh." I laugh. "Oops. Sorry. I just decided to walk home. It's such a nice day."

"It is lovely out. I was in the garden for a bit, but I spent most of the day reorganizing and cleaning out drawers so you and your dad will have all the space you need." She takes a sip from her mug of tea. "How was school?" she asks.

"It was good!" I chirp, staring into the pantry for a snack. "My Advisory teacher remembers Dad, and I made one friend so far, so yeah, all good stuff."

I sit down with her at the table and rip open a mini bag of pretzels.

She stares at me, almost looking shocked. "Wow, so happy to hear that!"

I finish crunching and ask, "Where's my dad, by the way?"

She sighs, and it feels like it takes her a long time to answer me. "I think he's lying down again. Oh, Natty. I'm worried about him: taking a medical leave from work, moving back in with his parents. This isn't how things are supposed to be."

"Grandma, it's gonna be okay. Seriously. I honestly feel like it's all really going to be okay. Better than okay. Really."

She shakes her head, not like she disagrees with me but more in a way that she's not sure how we'll get there, how things will feel okay again. She finishes her tea, drops the bag into the trash can, puts her mug in the dishwasher, and then sort of looks at me again.

"I spent some time researching synagogues today," she says. "Thanks to your mom, you were all much more active Jews than we ever were, and I'd hate for you to lose that here, but over the years the Jewish community has really dissipated, and the closest synagogue is a half hour away." She shakes her head. "There's so much to figure out, and I want things to be good for you here, and I'm just so worried—"

"Grandma!" I interrupt her, and stand up. "It's okay, really. It's going to be great. A half hour isn't that far. We'll figure it out!"

She sniffles. "I just love you so much." She pulls me

into a hug and keeps me there for a few seconds longer than I'd expect.

I walk into the den, where I find my dad lying on the couch, his mouth wide open, snoring away like it's the middle of the night. But it's not the middle of the night. It's four in the afternoon on a beautiful, sunny, warm September day.

I stand there for a moment, staring at him, and then realize it's good that he's sleeping. He's tired and weary and he needs to rest. We got here late last night and we were at school early this morning to fill out the paperwork. He's tired. It makes sense.

I head back to the kitchen and grab a can of seltzer and then go out to the front steps. Even though they're a little dilapidated and need to be painted, this is my favorite part of my grandparents' house. It's peaceful out here, and I like to look across the street and wonder about the people in all the homes. I've visited so many times, but I still don't really know their neighbors. My grandparents aren't close with them either.

Maybe that's one purpose I have here, to encourage a more friendly street. Maybe it'll help Dad, too. And then we can tell Mom about how great it is, and she'll want to be here even sooner. So many maybes, so many options.

I'm bursting with ideas, and I don't know where to start or what to do first. Probably my homework, but I'll get to that later. Right now, I want to live in the possibilities, the optimism, the idea that anything is possible, and yeah, maybe we've reached rock bottom, maybe my dad has reached the depths of despair, maybe my mom has, too, but that means we can only go up.

We can only go up from here.

I am one thousand percent sure of that.

ON THE WAY TO LUNCH the next day, I actually see a poster tacked onto one of the blank bulletin boards outside the main office.

It's on gray paper with a green cartoon frog and a big speech bubble that says:

JOIN A CLUB!

Creative Writing! Arts & Crafts! Debate!

Model UN! Or start your own!

Miller Creek Junior High ♥ clubs!

It has a little tear-off thing at the bottom with ten little slips that say, "Email Mr. Woodson for more information: bwoodson@mcjh.school."

I rip one off and put it into the front pocket of my back-pack.

Honestly, I hate to be critical, but what this school really needs is a bulletin board club. One boring flyer on a blank bulletin board? That's no good.

I walk into the cafeteria and scan the entire room, trying not to gag at the combination smell of floor cleaner and chili. It's pretty much what you'd expect: groups of kids scattered around, carrying ugly green lunch trays. Boys who pummel each other as they find seats; a group of girls all matching in the exact same cutoff jean shorts and white T-shirts, playing with their hair as they talk.

In the way back of the cafeteria, I see a table of kids who look like they don't fit in. They're wearing dark colors and chunky sweaters even though it's still sticky, hot September. Some of the girls have their hair in their faces—bangs that are too long but not because they're growing them out, probably because they like them that way. There are a few boys at the table, too.

That's where I'll go. This is no doubt the table of kids who look like they'd accept an outsider, someone new, someone who hasn't found her place yet.

Back in Willets, I ended up being part of the "popular girls"—we called ourselves The Core, which is so cringy now that I think about it—because we had all been best friends since kindergarten and we just sort of evolved into the popular girls. It's not like we tried to be that way; it just happened. But we definitely didn't let new people in. If I found that type of crew here—and I'm almost positive I already did: the girls in matching cutoff shorts—I'm pretty sure there's zero chance they'd let me sit with them.

In Willets, all of our moms became a crew at the first PTA meeting in kindergarten, so we just became a crew, too. I kind of think that's how it works sometimes. You just fall into stuff, and it sticks.

It all looked perfect, from a distance. And I guess it was kind of perfect for a while. Until it wasn't. Until my mom wasn't a smiley little PTA mom all the time, and then the rest of the moms weren't as interested in being her friend anymore. And then it trickled down to the daughters, too.

I push that all out of my head. It doesn't matter now. It's over. I'm here in this moment, and it's going to be great, and my mom's going to come, and Willets will be in the past, something I don't even think about anymore.

I walk through the rows in the cafeteria, and when I make it to that table, I realize there's an empty chair at the end. Perfect! It's like the seat is literally waiting for me.

"Hey!" I say, all excited, definitely sounding over-the-top, but in a good way, I think. "I'm Natty."

They stare at me in that way people do—from the bottoms of their eyeballs, like it's not worth the effort to look up and open their eyes the whole way.

"I just moved here," I continue. "My dad grew up here, though, so it's not like a totally foreign land." I laugh at myself, like it'll encourage them to laugh, too. But they barely even crack a smile.

So then I just sit back in my chair and open my lunch bag. It's sort of weird that Grandma makes my lunch now. Like she probably figured that phase of her life was over, but here she is, making school lunches again. She asks me what I want and stuff, but I don't want to make more work for her, so so far I've just had the same turkey, American cheese, and drop of mayo on whole wheat bread. Plus a pink lady apple (my favorite) and a small bag of kettle chips.

But today, when I dig down to the bottom of the bag, I find something else. A stack of thin chocolate chip cookies wrapped in tinfoil. I didn't know Grandma was baking again.

It's a bad sign. It seems like it should be the opposite. Like how could baked goods be bad? But Grandma only bakes when she's stressed. Like, really, really stressed. I bet she was up late baking, worrying about Dad and worrying about me and our life here.

"Whoa, you bring homemade cookies for lunch?" one of the girls shrieks. She has the farthest side part I've ever seen and tight, spiral curls.

"I didn't realize I did." I laugh again. "My grandma bakes when she's stressed, so clearly she's really, really stressed."

They look at me half confused, half like they don't care.

"Want one?" I ask.

"Um, yeah," extreme-side-part girl says, spreading her hand across the table like she's trying to display her sad school-lunch tray. "Sorry none of us said hi when you told us your name," she goes on. "We hate people, just FYI. So if you also hate people, you've found the right table. And welcome."

I slow-nod. I don't really know how to respond to that.

"I'm Lilian, but no one calls me that," she continues. "I prefer Luna."

I smile. "Luna is nice. I love the moon."

"I think of it more like the goddess," she replies. "But yeah."

"Yeah, well, moon goddess." I nod. "Very cool."

"My friends won't introduce themselves, so I'll do it for them," Luna continues. "That's Wade, Tape, and Braid."

I nod, realizing I need to find a quick way to remember

all of their names. Luna will be easy since her nickname is so distinct and so is her side part. And Wade makes me think of a wading pool and his eyes are crystal blue like pool water. That'll work. Braid is obvious because she has one long skinny braid and Tape . . . hmm. Well, Tape is unique and also not really a name, but she does have earrings made of duct tape, so I guess that has something to do with the nickname.

They all stare at me and poke at the cafeteria chili with plastic sporks, and I start to realize that a spork is actually kind of genius and a very underrated utensil. It's sort of rare to see a spork, and even rarer to appreciate it.

"Are you named for someone named Lilian?" I ask after a bite of my turkey sandwich to try and keep the conversation going.

"Yeah, my great-aunt. She was kind of a miserable woman, though, and hated everyone and I think everyone also hated her, so unclear why I was named for her." She shrugs, picking off another piece of cookie. "But I clearly inherited her hatred of people, soooo, yeah."

"That's confusing, but think of it this way—you can fully reclaim the name." I pause, realizing I'm saying the wrong thing. She hates her name. She wants to be Luna. Not sure why I went down this path. "I mean, I know you hate it, and that's fine, but also, like, you'll change it and future generations will think Lilian is awesome. I guess what I'm saying is we can always change things for the better even if people in the past weren't ideal."

Luna's eyebrows crinkle together, like she's confused but also thinking about it, like we've made a tiny connection somehow, already.

"Wait, what's your name again?" Luna asks, finally, after she finishes the whole cookie.

"Natty."

"Is that your actual name or a nickname?" she asks.

"It's short for Natanya. But Mom called me Natty since I was a baby and it stuck and now pretty much everyone I've ever met calls me that."

"Cool." She smiles. "I've never heard the name Natanya before."

"Yeah." I shrug. "It's Hebrew. My mom studied abroad in Israel in college and kind of became obsessed with Israeli culture."

"Wait. You're Jewish?" Wade asks, jumping into the conversation.

I nod and feel my face prickle a little. The way he says it, so surprised sounding, it just feels weird.

"We used to have a Jewish family in our grade. These twin girls; they were nice," Luna explains. "But they moved away last year. I think you're the only Jewish kid in the grade now."

"Oh, um, well, I can represent the tribe." I laugh.

The rest of the lunch period is pretty quiet. I finish my sandwich and smile when people look up at me, and I feel fine at this table.

All in all—a good first attempt.

I'm on a path with Luna—she's as different from The Core as she could possibly get, but she said my name was cool and she seemed nice.

Definite friend potential.

5

GRANDPA DECIDES THAT SINCE IT still feels like summer he's going to grill tonight: burgers and hot dogs and corn. And Grandma buys potato salad and coleslaw from the deli counter at the grocery store. She's the kind of person who doesn't move the salads to fancy bowls or anything. She puts them out in the containers and sticks spoons in them, and that's it.

It's like all the effort she puts in is in the planning and prepping, not in the presentation.

But Grandpa puts the burgers and hot dogs on this silver tray, and I set the table outside. And when we sit down to eat, it looks festive and nice. Like maybe it could even be a small party if you didn't know any better.

While I'm waiting for dinner to be ready, I think about the flyer, wondering if someone who just moved here can really just start a club. It might be trying too hard, but I still kinda sorta want to start something. I decide to text Gracie and hopefully get some feedback.

Me: Gracieeeee my girl how are you

Gracie: OMG Natty I miss you beyond

Me: I miss youuuuuu beyonddddddd

Gracie: I thought you already forgot about me since you didn't text before bed last night

Me: NO WAY

Me: I COULD LITERALLY NEVER FORGET YOU

Me: I need your help though . . .

Gracie: ??

Me: is it weird to start a club since I just got here

Gracie: ummmm yeah, tbh that's a very Natty thing to do

Me: haha ikr

Gracie: yes

Me: sooo ideas?

Gracie: well, like what does the school need

Me: ummmm

Me: the bulletin boards are kinda lame and empty and not decorated

Me: Bulletin board club?

Gracie: lol that's kind of boring, no offense

Me: kk

Me: that's kinda what I thought

Gracie: dance club?

Me: maybe

Me: I gg have dinner

Me: will keep thinking, thx for your help

Gracie: xoxoxo

"This little barbecue is so nice!" I say when we're all at the table, spreading the paper napkin on my lap. "Grandpa, you were right; it totally feels like summer, and I'm glad we're stretching it as long as we can."

Grandpa half smiles and nods. "Glad you like it, Nat."

Everyone is quiet after that, and I wish someone would say something. I don't want to feel like I'm the only one who talks around here.

My dad sits next to me, sort of slumped over his plate like an angry teenager. He looks too skinny and he hasn't shaved in I don't know how long. His blue collared shirt is wrinkly and stretched out.

I don't want to feel bad for him, but I do. He doesn't understand how changing his attitude could make such a difference in his life.

I turn a little toward him and say, "Dad, I have an idea—" but then Grandma waves her hand a little and shushes me.

"Natty," she starts. "Not now."

I shrug it off and put ketchup on my burger and mustard on my hot dog and eat three servings of the potato salad. Grandma even put out pink lemonade, which is a nice treat.

My dad eats in silence and then clears his plate and goes back to the couch to lie down. So I help Grandma and Grandpa bring everything else in.

Grandma turns to me when we're both at the sink and she says, "Natty, there's a club at school I want you to go to."

"Oh, yeah? I just saw a flyer about clubs!" It feels like Grandma just read my mind somehow.

She nods. "It's for kids with divorcing parents, and I spoke to the school social worker. It meets on Thursdays in the library and it sounds like it'll be helpful."

I put the last plate in the dishwasher. "But I don't need help and my parents aren't divorcing. But thanks for thinking of me." I smile.

"Natty," she says softly.

"I don't need help." I smile, ignoring the tight, twisty feelings in my stomach that seem to get worse the more Grandma talks. "I'm fine. Everything is fine. I get that Dad's sad now and Mom left and all of it, but I'm actually doing okay, and also I don't think they'll get divorced. I think it's a break. Mom even said she just needed time to think and I get that. People need breaks. Breaks are good.

Breaks are restorative. Breaks help us figure things out. Everything is all good, Grandma!"

Grandma sighs. "Please think about it."

I agree only because I can see how distressed she's getting and she's older now and distress isn't good for anyone, but especially not for old people.

I walk into the den to see if my dad's eyes are open and if they are I'm going to ask him if he wants to take a walk around the neighborhood. Maybe he'll want to stroll by the baseball field where he used to play in high school; maybe that'll cheer him up.

But when I get in there, his eyes are closed, and he's snoring again and there's no point in waking him up.

"I'm going for a walk," I yell from the front door.

"Okay, I really don't want you out so late," Grandpa says, looking up from his recliner where he's reading a smooshed-in paperback.

"It's still really early, Grandpa." I giggle.

"I don't need this stress!" He mutters to himself as I leave the room.

I head outside to do a loop around the neighborhood, trying to think of a club I could start, and on my walk, I see Mack sitting on a bench in the park, outside the field where a little-kids' baseball game is going on.

I look at her and she looks at me and I'm about to keep walking and not bother her when she says, "Oh, hey."

Her voice sounds the perkiest I've ever heard it, like she's actually excited to see me. "Natty, right?"

"Yeah! Hey!"

She stares at me for a moment and then says, "What are you up to? Out so late."

I look at my watch. "Um, it's only six fifteen."

She laughs. "I know. It was a joke. I make them sometimes."

"Right. Ha."

"Wanna sit or are you in a hurry?" she asks, picking at an inflamed mosquito bite just above her ankle.

"I'm not in a hurry." I smile. "Actually, can we go watch that game? Little kids playing sports is so so cute."

"It is?" Mack twists up her face.

"Come on; it'll be fun."

We make it over to the bleachers by the baseball field and there are two Little League teams playing. The Miller Creek team wearing green jerseys versus Matley, a town about ten minutes from here, with yellow jerseys.

"How cute are they?" I ask Mack. "Isn't Little League a spring thing, though?"

"I have zero clue." Mack shakes her head. "I don't even know why we're here."

We sit there and watch the game. It's the eighth inning, so there's not much left. I look around the bleachers and then back to the field and then this short little boy in a

Miller Creek jersey hits the ball so hard and so far, it's literally a home run!

"Oh my god!" I yell, bursting up from my seat in excitement. Somehow it seems like his mom is the only one paying attention. She starts cheering and then I join in. "Woo!" I yell, clapping like this is one of the best things I've seen in a really long time.

"Natty," Mack says, under her breath. "What are you doing?"

"Cheering! That kid just hit a home run!"

"Oh my god. Stop!" Mack hisses, but I ignore her.

I turn around to face the bleachers, "Did you all see that?" I yell. "Go Miller Creek! Woo!"

A few people nod and cheer with me, and others clap a little. This crowd needs to get more fired up! So after that, anytime anyone hits the ball or runs toward home, I stand up and cheer and little by little, the others join in with me.

Pretty soon, everyone in the bleachers is cheering, at least a little bit.

When the game ends, I feel a tap on my shoulder. "Thanks for cheering the kids on," Home Run Kid's mom says. "They can certainly use the support; this game was rescheduled three times due to rain and the season is technically over, but we wanted to make it happen."

"Of course! They're so cute, and I love cheering people

on." I shrug. "And we can *all* use some extra support!"

She smiles. "I agree."

"You're the weirdest person I've ever met," Mack says as we're leaving the park. "Who just randomly starts cheering at a Little League game like that?"

I shrug. "It was fun!" I look at my watch. "But I need to hurry home. My grandparents are gonna freak that I've been out this long."

We start walking faster, and Mack says, "I don't get it. Your dad grew up here, and now you just live with your grandparents? Why in the world would anyone who made it out ever want to come back here? And where's your mom?"

"It's a long story," I say. "Let's save it for another time. I'm kinda tired from all the cheering."

Mack shakes her head and laughs for a second. "Okay."

"Wait, there was something else I had to ask you, um . . ." I pause. "Oh! Where do you sit at lunch?"

"I don't sit. And I don't eat lunch."

"Huh?"

"The cafeteria food is gross, my mom refuses to make me lunch, and I hate all the kids in the school, so . . ."

I laugh. "I found the table of people who say they hate people. Luna is one of their names?"

"Oh, no way, they're awful, you can't sit there."

"Wait, why?"

Mack kicks a rock across the street. "Now that's

definitely too long a story. I gotta turn here to get home."
She hesitates, like she has something else to say but isn't
sure she should say it. "Good talking to you, though."

"Same." I smile, and a sort of satisfied feeling washes
over me, like when you finish putting in the last piece of
a jigsaw puzzle you've been working on for a week.

Mack suddenly doesn't seem to hate me as much.
Maybe she likes me, even. The tiniest bit.

6

I'M AT MY LOCKER AFTER school on Friday, putting books away and about to head to the bus line when I feel a tap on my shoulder.

"Lunch Girl, any interest in coming to scrub the basketball court with us?" Luna asks, her side part a little less extreme today. The other lunch table kids are standing behind her, holding buckets and sponges.

"Umm." I'm trying to figure out what she means by this, if it's some kind of joke or prank.

"Okay, starting over. Let me explain." She puts her hands on her hips. "We, um, so yeah, we vandalized the basketball court over the summer, and part of our punishment is to clean it up, and we can use all the help we can get, and you seem like a go-getter type, so . . ."

She lifts her shoulders, waiting for me to answer. It's

sort of an odd invitation, but I'm happy to hear she thinks I'm a go-getter type!

"Wait, you vandalized a basketball court at a school you hadn't even started yet?" I say, and wish I could take it back, realizing I may sound a little judgmental.

"Well, the elementary school and junior high share this basketball court. It's the same campus, basically." Wade drapes an arm over Luna's shoulder and joins the conversation. He seems to always speak like an almost-adult.

"So what exactly did you do to it?" I ask.

Tape jumps in to explain, adjusting a strip of duct tape on her forehead. "Mostly just spray-painted 'butt' in the corner of the court, popped a few basketballs in the supply bin, wrote 'butt' in permanent marker on the supply bin . . ."

I burst out laughing at the way she says "butt."

"So you in?" Luna asks again, and at that exact second, I feel my phone vibrating nonstop in my pocket. I try to take it out slyly to see who is texting me.

It's Gracie.

Gracie: Natty. Freaking out rn. I need to talk to you

Me: wdym? Explain

Gracie: with The Core. Major drama . . . Need to talk

Me: omg don't worry, whatever it is, it'll be okay, I promise

Me: YOU ARE AMAZING!

Gracie: Natty. For real.

"Hey! No phones out in school!"

I whip around and see a tall teacher with a skinny tie standing over me.

"Oh! Sorry! Putting it away!"

My face is on fire. I quickly shove my phone in my sweatshirt pocket. Gracie's gonna wonder why I'm not answering her.

"Ooh, Natty is definitely one of us!" Luna says, nudging me with her elbow. "Come with us. You can't say no now; you just got in trouble!"

"Lunch Girl! Breaking the rules!" Wade cheers. "But yeah, we need to get over there."

I follow the lunch crew down the hallway, sort of confused about what's going to happen, while at the same time feeling happy to be included in something here and also embarrassed that I just got in trouble for having my phone out.

"Natty, where are you going?" Mack says, passing us in the hallway. "The bus line is in the other direction."

"Oh, um, to the basketball court. I told, um, Luna and Braid and those kids I'd help them clean it up." I pull my hair into a ponytail. "I'll catch the late bus."

"Why are you helping *them*? You didn't vandalize anything, and they're awful. I told you that."

"I don't mind helping," I say, cheerful sounding.

"All right. It's your funeral."

I have to admit I've never fully understood that expression. It sounds grimmer than it is meant to, I think.

Mack keeps walking, and I run down the hallway a little to catch up to Luna and the rest of them.

But when we get out to the basketball court, we put down the buckets and sponges and stand there frozen for a second.

An actual basketball game is going on!

"This is just soooo Miller Creek," Braid says. "They tell us to come clean today, not even realizing an actual game is happening! I mean, seriously."

Wade shrugs. "Don't complain; at least we don't have to do anything."

"They don't even seem to care that they're playing on a court that says 'butt' on it," Tape sneers, and starts laughing.

I cover my mouth and laugh a little, too. I can't help it.

We're about to walk away when we hear a few random woos and lackluster clapping from some players on the sidelines. "A three-pointer!" one of them shouts. "Way to score, Miller Creek! This team is on fire!"

"We just scored a three-pointer!" I yell, like I actually understand basketball and know what I'm talking about.

"I don't know what that means," Tape says. "See y'all tomorrow."

We're picking up the sponges and buckets, about to head out, and then we see it with our own eyes: another three-pointer! I jump up and cheer. "Yeah! Woo! Go, Miller Creek!"

"Uh, Natty." Luna looks at me sideways. "What are you doing?"

"Cheering! Come on! Let's go watch the game. Seems like we're really good. And we have to wait for the late bus, anyway."

"Who is this girl?" Braid mutters.

Reluctantly, they all follow me to the rows of rusty folding chairs that only a few people seem to be sitting in. The school has bleachers but they're over by the track, which is on the other side of the school. Everyone else takes out their phones and sits there, half scrolling, half watching the game.

"We are actually, um, kind of good," Luna says, turning to face me a little.

"So good!" I leap up after another basket. "Yeah! Make that swoosh! Go, Miller Creek!"

"Ew, stop," Tape mutters under her breath. "This is so embarrassing."

I clap for a few more seconds and then sit back down and turn to Luna. "Want to try something?"

"Um, not really." She clenches her teeth like she's nervous about whatever I'm going to say. "Okay, what is it?"

"When I say Miller, you say Creek." I stand up and shout. "Miller!" And I motion for her to say, "Creek," but she covers her face with her hands and shakes her head like she needs me to stop or the world will implode.

I laugh to break up the awkwardness. "Okayyyyy, guess we'll try that again later."

"You're funny," Braid says, 60 percent compliment, 40 percent sarcasm.

I can't say I know a ton about basketball. Okay, I know nothing about basketball. But I watch the coach and the few other people in the seats, and when they clap, I clap, too, but louder, and I cheer and woo and do all the things people do when they're excited about a team.

"Yeah! Way to score!" Wade jumps up from his seat and shouts, mostly like he's making fun of the situation but maybe a tiny bit excited.

"Uh, Wade." I turn to him. "That was the other team."

He clenches his teeth and looks down. "Uh, yeah. I knew that."

We all crack up after that, and somehow the rest of the game flies by between cheering and clapping, Wade making random jokes, Tape muttering comments under her breath, and okay, I'll be honest, they're all mostly staring at their phones.

"Yeah! Woo!" I cheer and clap at the end. "Go, Miller Creek!"

"We just beat Northside forty-one to thirty-five!" I say to everyone as we're walking across the grass toward the late bus. "That was so fun!"

"Okay, wow. You clearly have a verrrrrrry different

definition of fun than we do," Tape says.

"Don't listen to her," Luna says. "She's just a hater."

"So you had fun?" I ask Luna.

"I didn't say that." She rolls her eyes. "Okay, I had a little fun. Like the tiniest amount."

"Oh my god!" I shriek, and then everyone stops walking. "That's the club!"

"What club?" Braid asks, annoyed sounding.

"The club I need to start! A pep squad!"

"Girl, you are from another planet." Luna shakes her head. "No one here wants to be on a pep squad. This is the least peppy place in the world. Couldn't you tell by, like, the three people who showed up to watch the game?"

"I know, but that's why we need it! And guess what?"

"Oh dear lord." Tape groans. "What?"

"I bet we can convince the school that if you do this, you won't have to clean up the basketball court, like it'll show you're taking initiative in a different way!" I shoulder-dance. "My old school would always go for stuff like that."

"Really?" Tape asks, taking the duct tape off her forehead and putting it on her arm.

"Wait, so you're saying you can get us out of cleaning . . . ," Braid mutters.

Wade kicks up some dirt with the toe of his Converse. "Okay, everyone, stop. I'm unclear on what is happening right now. I can't be on a pep squad!"

"Bro! She's gonna get us out of cleaning. . . ." Luna's voice trails off, and I honestly think I'm onto something! But it's more than that. All of a sudden, I feel pretty much the most excited I've ever felt. My fingers are all tingly and my heart is pounding in my head, and all I want to do is start this club right now. Like this second!

It won't even be that hard! We'll cheer for all the sporting events throughout the year. Maybe we can organize a pep rally! We'll have the best time! Plus it'll totally boost morale around here. Pretty soon Miller Creek will be the happiest place in the world, the place my mom *needs* to be.

That's it. There's no doubt about it.

I was born to start this club.

7

I HOP OFF THE LATE bus, run into the house, and dig
the little tear-off slip out of the front pocket of my backpack. It's a little soggy since my water bottle leaked, but
I straighten it out and luckily I can still see the email
address pretty clearly.

From: Natty Blaken
To: Mr. Woodson
Subject: Clubs!!!!!!!!!!!!!!!

Dear Mr. Woodson:

Hi! I'm Natty Blaken. I'm new here, and we
haven't met yet, but I saw your flyer about clubs
and I'm so excited and I want to start one! Here's
what I want to start: a pep squad!!!! I already

cheered on the basketball team today with the group of kids I sit with at lunch and I really think this club will be a great addition to the school!! Also, we went out there because those are the kids who are supposed to clean the basketball court, but if they join a club instead maybe they can be excused from cleaning? This worked in my old school on Long Island when a group of boys got into a food fight and poured baked beans on each other's heads and then they joined the social action club as a punishment, but it ended up being really great. Anyway, that's probably more info than you need, but please write back and let me know if I can start this club and if that works for their "punishment." I AM SOOO EXCITED ABOUT THIS.

Thank you!

Natty J. Blaken

I'm bursting after that, really hoping that Mr. Woodson will write back right away, but it's a Friday so who knows when he'll even see it. I may need to wait until Monday to get a response and that feels so hard. Actually impossible.

I need to start this club, like, now. It's the most sure I've ever been of anything in my whole life.

I refresh my email a thousand times and then it's

finally time for dinner. Grandma makes cheese quesadillas and guacamole and the avocados aren't really ripe enough yet, but it's still good. She always puts in the perfect amount of lime and that makes a huge difference.

It's kind of weird that it's a Friday and we're not having Shabbat dinner with all the blessings over the wine and the candles and the challah. It's just not a Grandma/Grandpa thing. It's a Mom thing. We'll get back to it, I'm sure. It'll just take some time. But at least we're all eating together.

"You guys are never going to believe the most amazing idea I had," I announce, dipping a chip into the guacamole.

"Hmm?" Grandpa looks up from his plate. For some reason he cuts his quesadillas into pieces with a fork and knife like he's eating a steak and it makes me laugh.

I look around the table to make sure Dad and Grandma are paying attention. They don't seem to be the most engaged I've ever seen them, but I think they're listening.

"Ready to hear this?" I crunch the tortilla chip and wait for them all to nod and look up. "I'm starting a pep squad at school!"

I smile wide and do a little clap for myself. Okay, yeah, it's sort of a lie since I haven't gotten approval yet or even heard back from Mr. Woodson and I emailed him less than two hours ago, and we only cheered at one game, but none of that matters!

Sometimes you just have to put positivity and confidence into the universe for everything to fall into place.

I sip my iced tea and say, "Some kids and I randomly stumbled upon a basketball game today—long story—and it was so fun to cheer for the team and I just think this club will be the best thing ever!"

Grandma nods. "Very interesting, Natty. I like how you're always thinking of ideas."

"She really does think a lot," Grandpa adds, and then shakes his head. "Do you get a headache thinking so much?"

"Never." I laugh. "Isn't that amazing, though? Like, the best idea you've ever heard?"

My dad dips his quesadilla into the lump of guacamole on his plate and then looks up at me. "Very cool, Natty." His tone doesn't really scream enthusiasm, but at least he's saying the right thing. It's okay, a step in the right direction.

"But seriously, it's, like, the best idea you've ever heard, though, right?" I smile and dip another chip into the guacamole. "I just think it's going to be so much fun, and we'll, like, make up cheers and routines and everyone will get so excited, and I think it's totally a way to make this town happier and the school peppier, and I mean, it's already great here, but it can be even better, and Mom will—"

Grandma puts her hand on my hand. "Wonderful,

Natty," she says softly, looking over at my dad. "I think we just need to have a little quiet now, though, okay, sweetie?"

"Um, yeah, totally." I take a sip of my iced tea. "Quiet dinners are great."

We sit in a thick silence after that and I try to go back to my quesadilla and my guacamole, but suddenly my stomach hurts too much to eat another bite. I can't even take another sip of iced tea. I want to go upstairs, but I know it's my job to clean up after dinner. So I sit there and smile, and I move the food around on my plate so it seems like I'm eating.

When everyone is done, I clear the table and load the dishwasher. Grandma stays with me in the kitchen and she wipes down the counters and waters her plants, but she doesn't say anything else, and then Dad leaves for Back to School night. It's kind of weird they have it on a Friday, but I guess they figure the teachers are off the next day so it's easier for them.

When I finally make it up to the attic, I change into pajamas and Google "how to start a pep squad." A few minutes into my research, my phone buzzes with a million texts from Gracie in a row.

Grace: Natty!

Grace: way to ghost me on text

Grace: where are you

Me: heyyyyyy

Me: wait what

Grace: I texted about drama with The Core and you just stopped writing

Me: omg yeah I got in trouble for texting in the hallway and then I got distracted

Me: I am sooo soo so so so so sorry

Grace: ok

Me: How are you

Grace: The Core is trying to kick me out I think

Me: I cannot believe that Gracie. For real. No way. You basically ARE THE CORE

Grace: Idk Natty. It's different now

Me: this feels impossible

Me: Want to FaceTime?

Grace: tomorrow, k?

Me: kk

Grace: xoxo

Me: XO!

I lay in bed that night with so many thoughts bouncing around my brain that it's pretty much impossible to fall asleep. At least I have an amazing view of the slim crescent moon from my little attic window.

Virtual silver lining to what I'm pretty sure will be a sleepless night.

I REFRESH MY EMAIL A thousand times over the weekend and then a thousand more times while eating breakfast before school on Monday morning. Still nothing from Mr. Woodson.

Now that I've come up with the most brilliant idea of my entire life, I just need it to be a thing already. The sooner I start it, the sooner it can be amazing, and the sooner my mom can get here to see the awesomeness.

"Natty, I couldn't sleep last night so I made those sugar cookies with the sprinkles you used to love," Grandma says with her back to me while doing dishes.

"Yum, thank you," I reply.

My phone starts vibrating in the middle of what feels like my three thousandth email refresh.

"Hi, Mom!" I answer.

"How's everything going, Nat?" she asks in her soft voice. I call this her yoga voice. It always sounds as if she's about to start a yoga class or has just finished one or is thinking about yoga. I can't explain it, but it really feels true to me.

"Everything is going great! I've met so many kids at school already, and they're all different but also really interesting. There's this girl Mack who is on the bus with me and then literally in every single class," I tell her. "And also I'm starting a—"

She interrupts me. "Oh, Nat. Wonderful. I'm really happy about this. Listen, I really can't talk long but I want to hear all about this soon. Just wanted to, um, say hello."

I laugh, my stomach tightening up again. "Oh, okay. Hello!"

"So listen, we'll talk soon, okay?" She pauses again, and it feels like someone is pulling her away.

"Yeah, definitely. Oh, by the way, Grandma's trying to find the closest synagogue to here so we can go to services and stuff, and then figure out my bat mitzvah. I forgot to tell you that the other day."

"Oh, really?" Her voice perks up. "That's wonderful."

"I know!" I smile, happy she's happy. "But when are you coming to visit? You said hopefully end of September, right? Time is flying by!"

She hesitates. "Well, I'm not sure when exactly. But hopefully soon."

"Are you still in Hawaii or—?" I force my voice to be upbeat and relaxed-sounding, casual, not like I'm nervous or unsure about where she is and what she's doing.

"Oh no, I'm back. That was just a short trip to clear my head. I'm staying with a friend in Brooklyn."

I smile. Brooklyn is way closer than Hawaii. That makes me feel a little better.

"Well, I really hope you can come soon. It's so good. So much different than just visiting, Mom. Really. It's just easy and relaxed and my Advisory teacher loves yoga, too!" I shriek.

"Oh, Natty. Wow, that's great." She clears her throat. "In the meantime, know that I love you. Up to the moon. Okay?"

"Up to the moon." I smile, rubbing my stomach, trying to get the knots to untwist. "Love you, Mom."

"Love you, Natty-girl."

Actually, her not coming to visit right away is kind of a good thing. It gives me more time to get everything set up with the pep squad and really solidify my friendships with Mack and Luna and the rest of the lunch table crew.

"Lunch Girl," Tape says, flat-sounding, as soon as I make it to the table in the cafeteria. Today she has a strip of duct tape making a collar on her black T-shirt. It actually looks kind of good.

"Hi!" I say as cheerful as possible. "So I know I don't

have the official approval yet, but if I get it, we can go and cheer at the first cross-country meet of the season. It's next week!" I do a little dance with my arms. "We'll try to perform at all the sports events or, uh, games or whatever you call them! And then I want to just have a regular pep rally, too!"

Luna squints. "Whoa, slow down. We don't even know if we can do this yet." She stabs her cafeteria meatball. "And what do you mean 'pep rally'?"

"It's like when the whole school gets together in the gym or outside on the bleachers, and we pump everyone up." I nod like this is a thing they should all be familiar with. "The high school in my old town had them, and they'd hang flyers all around town, and people could just come by if they wanted."

Braid says, "I've literally never seen or heard of that. I don't think that kind of thing exists in Miller Creek."

"Well, it will now! I mean, as soon as they say it's okay. . . ." I laugh.

"Uhhh, epic levels of enthusiasm, Lunch Girl," Wade mutters.

"Seriously. Where did she even come from?" Braid shakes her head.

"Ignore them," Luna says, stabbing her meatball again. "They just don't know what to do with people who have, like, actual energy."

"It's all good!"

The rest of lunch is quiet until Mr. Woodson comes to find me at the table and asks if he can talk to me outside.

"Ooooooh. Lunch Girl's in trouble," Braid sing-songs.

"Aw, Lunch Girl!" Tape shakes her head, laughing. "So disappointed in you."

"Okay, calm down." Mr. Woodson wipes some sweat off his forehead with the back of his hand. "She's not in trouble."

"So, Natty," he starts when we're outside the cafeteria. "I, um, got your email. And it's a lovely idea. You sure you're up for something like this, though? You just got here. It's unusual for someone new to start a club. . . ."

"Yes! Definitely! I was born to start this club!!" I smile. "What did you think about my other idea? For, um, my lunch table crew."

"Well, about that." He hesitates. "We can certainly try it, and I love that they'd be getting more involved in school. Anyone who participates in a club gets community service credit." He pauses. "The thing is, we'd have to make sure they really show up and participate. Otherwise they'll have to go back to cleaning. . . ."

"Oh yeah, totally." I nod. "They'll show up, don't worry! I can take attendance and stuff, but is there, like, a faculty adviser person assigned to each club?"

"Much of the faculty is overcommitted at the moment." He clears his throat. "I'll be here to help as much as I can. . . . I don't know much about pep squads but—"

"Don't worry at all. I have this figured out. I mean, when it's time to sign up for competitions and stuff, I may need some signatures from the school and help with forms, but I'll take care of everything else." I pause. "And you know, we may need to order stuff eventually but not yet. Maybe some supplies. But we'll figure it all out. Thank you so much, Mr. Woodson! Everything's going to be great."

His eyes sort of glaze over then, like maybe he didn't get enough sleep last night. "Okay, Natty." He soft-smiles and sighs. "Looking forward to it."

He starts to walk away, and I call out to him.

"Oh, Mr. Woodson, one more thing," I say, and he turns around. "Can I make an announcement about the first meeting? Like over the loudspeaker? So people know to come!"

"Great, just clear it with Sheila in the main office. Sound okay?"

"Sounds better than okay!" I smile. "Sounds great!"

9

AT LUNCH THE NEXT DAY, I recruit Luna to hang some pep squad meeting flyers with me.

"It's kind of nutty how we just met you and you've gotten us out of our punishment somehow," she says, pushing a thumbtack into the bulletin board. "You're kind of like a little miracle worker person."

"Yay! That's all I've ever wanted to be!" I smile. "I'm going to make an announcement about the meeting over the loudspeaker later. Want to come? Oh! Want to be my cocaptain?"

She widens her eyes. "Whoa, girl, whoa. Calm down! I need to see what this whole squad is about first."

"Fine," I groan. "But you're gonna love it."

After the last bell of the day rings, I rush down the

hall to the main office to see if I can make a last-minute announcement, and I run into Ms. Lamlot. Literally. Like, she's not paying attention, and she nearly slams her head into mine. She's very petite and we're almost the same height.

"Oh, Natty! Hi! So sorry!"

"It's okay." I pause. "Oh, Ms. Lamlot, we missed you in Advisory today."

"You're sweet, Natty. Every so often, we all need a little extra time." She pauses. "Isn't that right?"

"I agree. Yes." I smile, inching away a little; I need to make this announcement!

"It was lovely getting to chat and reunite with your dad at Back to School night," she says in a soothing, quiet tone. "You've all been through quite an ordeal."

"Oh, um, yeah, but we're fine," I stammer, ignoring the twisty pretzel feelings in my stomach. "I'm doing great, loving the new adventure!"

She nods, her chamomile-tea smile forming on her face.

I keep walking and wondering about Ms. Lamlot. Something seemed off with her, like she's distracted or overwhelmed. I'm not sure.

"Hi," I say to Sheila in the main office, out of breath. "I, um, just wanted to make a quick announcement."

"Go right ahead." She slides the little microphone thing

across the desk and doesn't look up from her magazine. "Just push the button and talk."

"Hiiiii, Miller Creek Junior High!" I say. "I'm Natty and I just wanted to tell everyone that the first-ever Miller Creek Junior High Pep Squad meeting is happening in the gym, um, right now. Actually, in five minutes! Come and find out what we're aaalll about! And get community service credit, too! Woo! Yay! K, thanks! Bye!"

"Good job." Sheila smiles in a sort of forced kind of way, like she can't wait for me to be out of here.

I leave the office and flip my head over and pull all of my hair into a bun so it's off my neck. It's suddenly a thousand degrees in this school. I start running down the hall to the gym when Mack catches up to me. "You're actually starting a pep squad? For real?"

"Yes! And I am so excited!" I say. "You should come! Why are you rushing home?" I pause when the best idea ever pops into my brain. "Oh my god, Mack! You can be the mascot! No one will know it's you, and you can be in the club with me, and it'll be our secret!"

Mack hits my arm with the marble notebook she's holding. "Natty! What is wrong with you? Miller Creek doesn't have a mascot. What would it be? Hmmm. A disgruntled person who can't find work and is forced to eat canned beans every night for dinner?" She throws her head back, fully cracking up at her own joke. At least she's laughing. "Actually, I guess it's the frog. We are technically called the Miller Creek Frogs."

I laugh. "Just come to the meeting. You know you'll be lonely on the bus without me."

"Um, you're aware those delinquents you decided to befriend have been in classes with me since kindergarten and we all hate each other, right?" She pauses, waiting for me to respond.

"I'm so curious about why, though," I reply.

"I don't care if you're curious." She shrugs. "I hate every single person in this school and also the town, except for maybe Mrs. Guidcraft, the eighty-seven-year-old library clerk who reshelves all the books."

"Oooh, I haven't met her yet! I really want to, though. She sounds awesome."

"I hate you the most," Mack says, walking away, probably to put something away and grab stuff from her locker.

"Love you, Mack!" I yell out down the hall.

The cutoff girls all walk by then, and they stop at the bulletin board to look at my flyer.

"Why do we suddenly have a pep squad?" one of them squeaks. "It's like a TV show from the nineties or something."

"Ter, you don't know a single thing about the nineties," another one squeaks in the exact same tone.

"Should we go?" another one asks. "Since Two Step

closed, I've been really wanting to get back into dance, and this could be a really good way, and it won't cost money. At least I don't think it will."

"I am definitely not going," one replies. "You guys do whatever you want."

I shrug it off, because I know this squad won't appeal to everyone, and that's okay.

Mr. Woodson's already in the gym when I get there.

"Mr. Woodson! Hi!"

"Oh, hi, Natty," he says, defeated sounding.

"Are you okay?" I ask.

"Oh yeah, fine." He smiles. "Just juggling many things. You know how it is. Life, work, family . . . Taking it one day at a time. You know." He shakes his head, "Oh, I have no idea why I'm telling you all this."

I giggle. "Adults always tell me this kind of stuff. Especially my grandma. I think I give off a good-listener vibe. I'm kind of proud of that, actually."

"Yes. I think that's what it is." He must feel a vibration because he pulls his phone out of his pocket and answers it, and then holds up a finger, signaling to me that he needs to step away for a moment.

Soon all the kids from the lunch table get here, and a minute later, a few of the cutoff girls show up, too! Shock of the century.

And then a little while later, I see Mack coming in.

"I'm not joining whatever this is," she calls out. "I'm

just here to finish homework on the bleachers. The library was full."

"Well, it's lovely to have you here!" I yell back. "No matter what the reason is!"

She rolls her eyes and shakes her head so furiously it could almost fall off.

The rest of the kids are all sitting around in their little groups, chatting with each other, but time is ticking away, and I need to get this started.

Mr. Woodson is still on his call outside the gym and I'm not sure if I should start the meeting or not. I look over at him and try to make eye contact, but he doesn't see me.

I guess I don't have a choice. I have to start.

"Hi, everyone!" I yell so loud, and then start dancing around, bouncing from foot to foot.

"What is she doing?" Braid leans over and asks Wade, loud enough for me to overhear.

"So excited you're all here! We are making history! Right this moment! The first-ever Miller Creek Junior High School Pep Squad STARTS NOW!!!!!"

I turn on the playlist I made and "Get Ready for This" blasts from the tiny speaker on my phone.

I start doing jumping jacks and dancing around and motioning with my arms for everyone to get up and dance, too.

"I need you all to get up! Get up out of your seats!" I

yell. "Clap your hands! Dance around! Show your spirit! Show your pride!" I pound my fist in the air as I bop around. "Go! Go! Go!"

They all ignore me, but I keep dancing.

"If we're going to get up and dance, this should count as our gym class for the day, too," Wade says. "Can we get credit for that? Can we ask Woodson? Where is he anyway?"

I ignore him and I'm out of breath, so I have to stop dancing. I pause for a second—inhale and exhale—and then look down at my clipboard list of notes. I don't know what it is, but when I have a clipboard, I feel even better about myself. Like I'm truly the Natty I was born to be.

"Okay, everyone, next time you actually need to get up from your seats! But I'll count that as an observational exercise." I laugh. Mr. Woodson comes back into the gym and sits down on the rusty folding chair in the corner.

"Our first order of business is to learn everyone's names, so yeah, let's, um, go around and introduce ourselves and tell us your grade and your favorite, um, ice cream flavor?" I lift my eyebrows. "I'll go first. I'm Natty. I'm in seventh grade. My favorite flavor is chocolate chip cookie dough."

Then the lunch table crew goes.

"Luna. Seventh. Mint chip."

"Wade. Seventh. Toffee crunch."

"Braid. Seventh. I'm lactose intolerant and don't eat ice cream."

"Tape. Seventh. I'm vegan and don't believe in ice cream. Even dairy free."

"Thanks," I say. "All good answers." I motion my head toward the cutoff girls so they can go.

"Hiiiii! I'm Kingsley," says the girl with the pigtails. "I'm in seventh. My favorite flavor is vanilla. Boring. LOL." She giggles.

Kingsley with pigtails. King and pig sort of rhyme. That's how I'll remember her name.

"I'm Rowan, also seventh. Pistachio-o-o-o-o!" She shouts the last part like she's at a sporting event and there's an echo.

Row like rowboat, like a giant canoe? I guess it works since she's waaaay taller than the other two.

"Interesting choice," I reply.

"Hi. Terra. Seventh." Hmmmm. I can't think of a quick way to remember her name. Will need to think on that one. "Also can I say this is an amazing idea for a club, but why are only seventh graders here?"

"Eighth graders are smarter than we are," Braid jumps in.

"Okay." I clap. "Moving on. Terra, your favorite flavor?"

"Oh yeah." She laughs. "Coffee. Hands down. I love coffee ice cream."

"Wonderful. Thanks so much for sharing."

Braid stands up. "So what's the game plan here? I need to pick my baby cousin up at day care and take him home. Soooo . . . I'm kind of on the clock."

"Well, there's a cross-country meet on Monday! We have to be there! We'll make posters and cheer and it'll be great!"

"She is literally on another planet," Tape says, loud enough for everyone to hear.

"I finally agree with you on something, Theresa," Kingsley says, shooting eye-daggers at Tape and obviously calling her by the name she doesn't use. "Also I think you're wrong about it being on Monday 'cuz there's a cross-country meet going on right now. . . . My brother's on the team. I need to go meet my mom there."

Kingsley grabs her backpack and the whole group gets up to leave, like just because Kingsley's heading out, the meeting's somehow over.

"Wait!" I shout. "Let's go cheer on the team NOW! We don't need to wait! This is perfect! Forget talking about this, let's just DO this!"

"Um, what?" Braid asks. "Right now? This was just supposed to be a meeting!"

"Braid. Stop." Luna shakes her head. "Just give it a chance!"

"Yes! Give it a chance!" I pump my arms in the air in

front of me as I lead everyone out of the gym toward the track. "I want this club to be what you guys want it to be, too! I mean, look. I know we're all getting credit for being here, and it's serving a different purpose for all of us, but I think it can end up being even more than we realize. . . ."

"Oh, here we go, motivational speaker," Tape says, adjusting the piece of duct tape she has across her chin.

We get out to the track and it seems like the meet is actually not on the track, which is I guess how it works with cross-country. It just sort of starts and ends there. But that's okay. There's a staggered start time, so some runners haven't started yet.

"So now what do we do?" Kingsley asks, putting Rowan's hair into pigtails so they'll be even more matchy-matchy.

"Just cheer!" I smile. "Like this." I take a deep breath. "Go, runners! Go, Miller Creek! Yeah! Miller Creek Cross Country! Woo! Woo!"

"Wow." Wade widens his eyes. "Now that is epic-level enthusiasm."

"Don't we need, like, choreographed dances if we're a pep squad, though?" Rowan asks.

I bounce from foot to foot. "Yeah, of course! We'll get there. For now, just cheer!"

I look over at the lunch table crew, all slumped over

each other on the grass. "Come on, Lunch People, up! Everyone!"

"Theresa!" Tape's mom shouts from the bleachers, standing up. "What a wonderful thing! You joined a cheering squad!"

"Ew, Mom. Stop." Tape glares at me. "This is hell."

Well, at least a mom appreciates me!

I keep cheering while putting on the first song on my pep squad playlist, "Cheerleader" by Omi. It's not so loud through the tiny phone speaker on my phone, but it'll be okay.

"'Oh, I think that I found myself a cheerleader!'" I shout, trying to link arms with Rowan and Kingsley who are next to me. "Come on! Sing!"

"This is soooo embarrassing," Rowan says.

I look around, not sure how she could be embarrassed, since there's, like, no one even here to be embarrassed around!

"I actually love this song," Luna says, inching between Rowan and me.

"'She is always right there when we need her.'" We sing together, link arms, and kick our legs out in front of us, almost Rockette-style.

Then, as each runner finishes the event, Luna and I yell as loud as possible! "Woo! Yeah! You did it! Miller Creek rules!" Sometimes the others join in, but most of the time they stand there with all of their weight on one foot, lazily clapping, like this is among the worst things they've ever been part of.

"Um, hey." I feel a tap on my shoulder and turn around to see who it is.

I look down at his feet, and then I notice his shirt: Birkenstocks. Waffle House tee.

It's Running Kid from the first day!

"Hey!"

"Sooooo I basically only came here to watch people run and feel the satisfaction that I was seated and not running . . . but then I saw your little pep squad in action, and I feel like I kind of want to be part of it. . . ."

"You do?" I look at him sideways, unsure if he's kidding or being serious.

"Yeah, dude. I need to finish my comm serve credit so I can graduate eighth grade, and I think this will count . . . and I'm intrigued."

He sort of talks like he's surfing on a beach in Malibu, all slow and thoughtful, with his hand on his chin like maybe an old professor or something. He gives emphasis to each and every syllable.

"Well, great! Our next rehearsal is tomorrow. So come!"

"I. Will. Do. That," he says in a robot voice, laughing at himself.

Running Kid (I need to learn his name) walks away and I stop for a second to fix my bun. He actually wants to join the squad! For real!

When the meet ends, Braid turns to me and says, "Okay, wow, no offense, Lunch Girl, but we may need to reconsider just doing the cleaning instead. That was brutal."

"What? No." I laugh.

"Braid. Calm down. It'll be better when we have, like, an actual routine and stuff," Luna says, jumping into the conversation. "This is just the first day!"

I add, "Oh, yeah, totally, this wasn't planned *at all* and we honestly did pretty great, considering."

Braid replies, "Whatever you say . . ."

We make it back to the gym and I tell everyone to sign the sheet on the clipboard by the door so I have an email list for announcements and stuff.

I see a few of them scribbling something down, but when I walk over to see, it's the word "Butt" three times and the email is "butts@buttttttttttttttts.com."

I shake my head and tear the paper off the clipboard and throw it into the overflowing trash can by the door.

"They're all terrible," Mack says, after reading over my shoulder. "Do you believe me now? Can't believe you actually thought you were gonna get them to do this."

"No and no way." I smile, actually feeling pretty good about how today went. "Luna seemed kind of into it, actually. And a lot of them cheered! So what if they walked out and gave me fake emails? This was the first day. It takes time to convince people of stuff!"

"Um, yeah, clearly I haven't had any success convincing you that you're wrong about everything."

I don't respond to that.

There's nothing at all that can ruin my good vibes from today.

From: Natty Blaken
To: Mr. Woodson
Subject: PEP RALLY!!!!!!!!!!!

Dear Mr. Woodson:

We cheered on the cross-country team today and it was so awesome! I was thinking that we should pick a day for a pep rally when the whole community can come together. When would be good for that? I'm ready to start planning! I LOVE THIS CLUB!

Thanks for your help,

Natty J. Blaken

As soon as I finish my email to Mr. Woodson, I get a thousand texts from Gracie.

Gracie: Natty I have no clue what's happening.

Gracie: seriously freaking out

Gracie: everyone hates me all of a sudden

Me: what? No way. You're Gracie Ella Bover-Wilson. EVERYONE LOVES YOU

Gracie: Stop with that. I swear. I am being ICED OUT.

Me: Literally no way, I don't believe it.

Me: Just be your cheerful, positive self and it'll all be fine!

Me: GOOD VIBES ONLY!

Gracie: I'll FaceTime u later

Me: kk

Gracie's the kind of person who is so over-the-top sensitive that if people aren't totally obsessed with her, she thinks they hate her. It's kind of always been this way. And that's why she was the kindest to me when everything happened with my mom and The Core moms and then with me and The Core.

Having a little distance from the whole thing makes it a little easier to understand but that's not what I want to do. I don't want to waste my time dwelling on the past and stuff that's over and doesn't matter anymore.

"Hi, Mom," I say through the phone a little while later, pushing the Gracie text out of my head.

"Oh, hi, Natty." Her voice sounds asleep. "I just woke up from a nap."

I look at the clock. It's not even six p.m. yet.

"Nice. Sleep is good. Listen, I just wanted to tell you that there's this new inn in Miller Creek. It just opened. I passed it today on the bus. I think they're going for something like a quaint bed-and-breakfast vibe and it's the perfect place for you to stay when you come visit, if you feel weird staying at Grandma and Grandpa's. Not that you should feel weird; you're totally welcome. But just in case. Anyway, I could stay there with you; it would be really fun. Like a sleepover." I pause. "And it would be amazing if you could come this weekend. I know it's last minute, but on Monday you can see this pep squad I started. We're just getting going so we may be a little clumsy, but I also think it's gonna be awesome. I mean, I know it'll be awesome. I want you to be there when it starts so you can see how it evolves, and there's this inn and I know you love inns, soooo . . ."

I know it's bold of me to tell her to come so soon after starting the squad, but sometimes you have to be bold. Envision the scenario you want, and make it happen.

"Natty-girl, I love you so much, and I can't be there Monday. I promise I will be there as soon as I can." She's quiet then for what feels like five full minutes. "Okay, sweetie?"

I swallow hard. "Yeah, totally. It'll give me more time

and it may book early anyway, so it probably would have been hard to get a reservation." I lean back against the wall.

"Okay, we'll see, Natty-love." She sighs. "I think I'm going to go lie down again. Let's talk soon. Mama loves you."

I look across the attic, through the teeny, tiny window at the almost-getting-dark sky and I imagine her looking up at the same sky and it feels like we're actually not so far apart from one another. Brooklyn to Pennsylvania is very, very close when you think about it.

"Love you, too."

I try to ignore the fact that my stomach hurts again. I should probably see a doctor about it, but I don't want to give Dad something else to worry about.

Plus it's not like it hurts all day every day. It's on and off.

And besides, everything is good. If I was still living on Long Island, going to Willets, I'd never be starting a pep squad, I'd never have met Mack or even Luna and the others. I'd just be the same old Natty who's always been there, trying to figure things out with The Core, being pushed aside, further and further away from the way things used to be.

When my mom's depression started to get really bad, my dad and I got so sad, too. I mean, of course we did, but that didn't help her. I think it made things worse, actually. We all retreated from the community and felt more and more isolated.

It took a while to realize this, but now I see that spreading positivity is the way to go. Positivity breeds positivity! No sense in focusing on the bad stuff!

That night at dinner, Dad seems perky and more put-together. He's wearing a navy polo and khaki pants and it looks like he actually ironed them.

"So, apparently, I need to head over to Miller Creek Junior High *again*," my dad announces after he finishes a bite of meat loaf. "The other night was Back to School night and tonight we have curriculum night. I don't really understand the difference and why they're so close together and I definitely don't remember you guys having to go to so many meetings and events when I was a kid."

"I don't remember any meetings," Grandma muses. "Do you, Clark?"

"What?" Grandpa yells. "I can't hear you!"

"Grrrr," Grandma says. "I think I may need to make an appointment to get you evaluated for hearing aids."

"Good idea, Mom." Dad wipes the corners of his mouth with his napkin. "Well, team, this has been lovely, and I'm off to learn all about Natty's classes, so I will see you all tonight, maybe in the morning depending on how late this goes."

"It's curriculum night," Grandma scoffs. "How late could it go?"

"You never know." My dad laughs.

He leaves the table and then the house and I help Grandma load the dishwasher. Grandpa tells us he's going to work at fixing the wobbly dresser in the attic, the one I've been using, but I have a feeling he'll stop at his recliner on the way and end up dozing off.

I'm putting the last plate in the bottom rack when I feel my phone buzzing in my hoodie pocket.

"Oh, Grandma, it's Gracie FaceTiming. Can I take this?"

"Sure can." She smiles.

I let the phone buzz a few more times until I make it out to the deck so I can talk without disturbing anyone.

"Gracie!" I squeal. "How are you?"

"Terrible without you!" She makes a frowny face. "I miss you so much. Can you please move back?"

I scratch an itch at the back of my head. "Um, I don't know. My plan is to convince my mom to move here, so I'm working on that. . . . You'll come visit. It'll be great!"

"Wait. Hold up." She moves the phone closer to her face. "Are you serious? I thought this was like a temporary thing while your mom figured stuff out and went to Hawaii for that volunteer thing or whatever. You're really planning to live the rest of your life before college in Miller Creek? What about your bat mitzvah?"

"Well, we're figuring that out, there's still time, thanks to my late birthday, phew," I say. "But Gracie, honestly, Long Island was, like, not the best place for my mom. Way too materialistic. I think that may have been partly what caused the depression. And being here, it's like a whole new world to explore."

"Natty! This is me you're talking to." She lifts her eyebrows. "Please. You can be real with me. I've known you since kindergarten. You guys loved Willets until, well, you know, until your mom started to not feel great."

"Gracie, it's all good, though! I like it here! It's really all good."

She rolls her eyes, and then her dachshund, Arlo, hops onto her lap. "All you say is, 'It's all good.' What does that even mean?" She pauses. "You don't need to pretend everything is fine, Natty. For real."

"But everything is fine!" I laugh. "Anyway, let's change the topic. Tell me about other stuff. How's everything with Jake Wexner? Is he still so cute?"

"He's okay. Not as cute as he used to be. He grew his hair out and I'm not into it," she answers, but her heart doesn't seem to be into this conversation. "I had other stuff about The Core that I wanted to talk to you about, but I gotta go start this math homework. I may be up until three in the morning."

"Whoa. I hope not." I pause. "I'm here to talk whenever, here to listen, too."

"Natty, I love you so much, and I'm here for *you*, too. Okay? Just remember that."

"Well, of course. I could never forget that."

She blows me a kiss, and I blow one back, and then we end the call.

Thinking about Gracie being up all night working on math makes me realize I need to start my homework, too.

I definitely don't want to be up all night.

From: Mr. Woodson
To: Natty Blaken
Subject: RE: PEP RALLY!!!!!!!!!!

Natty,

I love this idea. I'll get a date on the calendar.
Thinking it should be sooner rather than later for
momentum and school spirit. Let's plan on the
second Monday in October.

MCJH is so lucky you moved here.

Mr. Woodson

"So was it always, like, your dream to start a pep squad
or something?" Mack asks me on the bus the next day.

"I mean, not exactly, but I just feel like we need more pep around here, and after we cheered on that Little League game, it was sort of one of those light bulb moments." I stare out the window at a leaf falling slowly to the ground. "Have you given any more thought to being the mascot?"

"Nope, not one more second of it. I love you, but I'm not doing it." Mack puts her knees up against the seat in front of us.

"You love me?" I shriek. "For real?"

"Stop it, Natty." She rolls her eyes at me and turns sideways, to face the aisle a little more.

We're quiet for a few minutes before Mack asks, "So do you miss your old school and old friends and stuff? You never tell me anything about your old life. It's weird."

"I mean kind of, a little, I guess, but I really feel like I'm where I'm supposed to be now. There's no point in missing stuff. Plus I think my mom'll end up moving here. I think the pep squad will help convince her."

"Huh? That makes literally no sense." She shakes her head, like she's too tired to continue this conversation. She offers me her bag of trail mix, the kind with the M&M'S in it. "Want some? It's actually very filling."

"No, thanks. I had breakfast before I left for the bus."

"Oooh, fancy." She rolls her eyes. "Did I tell you we might have to actually move?" she asks me.

"Away from Miller Creek?" I gasp, shocked.

"No, doof. Out of our falling-down, dilapidated catas-trophe of a house. I mean, I love it because it's mine and I've always lived here, but I think we have to move because the landlord is going to sell it. No clue how since it's a literal garbage dump, like, actually the dump is behind it." She stops talking. "Did you know that?"

I shake my head.

"Oh yeah, the Miller Creek dump, where people take big items that the trash department won't pick up and who knows what else—maybe like dead squirrels, ew—is literally my backyard."

"I didn't know we lived so close to the dump. . . . My grandparents actually have a lot of stuff to dispose of." I pause and think for a moment about how I'd take that broken Nok Hockey set over there. "Also, makes for some interesting people watching, I bet. . . ."

"Ignoring that. Anyway, yeah, so the landlord decided he wants to sell, and we can't afford to buy a house, obviously, so . . . And my dad doesn't have a job so no clue how we'll get another place, but my grandma has a friend who works at the rental office for that town house community near the train." She shrugs. "So we may move there."

"Town house community sounds fabulous. Like, with a clubhouse? And community events? And a pool for everyone to share?" I feel all fluttery thinking about it.

I miss the Willets neighborhood pool. It's fall now so I wouldn't be swimming, anyway, but Fourth of July there was my favorite day of the whole year.

"Um, Natty. There's one pool in Miller Creek. It's indoors at the basement of the senior center and it's used for aqua aerobics and that's it."

I'm about to tell her I actually love aqua aerobics, but I stop myself.

I'm getting better at the whole reading-a-room thing.

We get off the bus, put our jackets in our lockers, and then Mack and I walk together to Advisory.

"Natty!" Luna says as soon as she sees me, turning onto the B wing. "I have an amazing idea."

"Really?" I ask. "What is it?"

"Come on, Natty, no time, we need to go." Mack says through her teeth, grabbing my arm and pulling me down the hallway. "And not talk to her," she mutters under her breath.

I try to stop, but Mack keeps pulling me.

Luna rolls her eyes. "Emailing you right now," she calls out.

When we get to Advisory, Ms. Lamlot is waiting by the door, greeting everyone. She has a string of daisies in her hair and her cheeks are flushed pink, like she has just the right kind of blush on or she was recently embarrassed.

"Girls! Hi!" She smiles and then looks right at me. "Natty! How *are* you?"

"Um, I'm great, Ms. Lamlot, thanks for asking. How are you?"

"Wonderful, wonderful. Beautiful day, isn't it?"

"For sure. Fall weather is the best. Crisp and perfect."

I head to my desk, and when I get there, Mack rolls her eyes at me and then nudges her head in Ms. Lamlot's direction.

"She hates me," she mouths. "And I hate her."

"Oh, Mackie Mack," I say.

"Never call me that again."

"Noted." I tap the tip of my finger against my left temple.

"So, good morning. Welcome, students." Ms. Lamlot smiles. "Since this is Advisory and we all need a little extra time to catch up on things in the morning, feel free to study for tests, finish homework, meditate for the next fifteen minutes or so."

Everyone claps for that, and when Ms. Lamlot goes back to her desk, I ask if I can check something quickly on my phone. I want to see whatever Luna emailed!

"Of course, Natty." She smiles a sort of I-feel-bad-for-you smile, but I ignore it. "Whatever you need."

So I grab my phone from my backpack front pocket and walk out into the hall and I open my school email.

From: Lilian Ward
To: Natanya Blaken
Subject: PEPPPPPPP

Natty!

I had an amazing idea. Me and you should meet separately to come up with dances and choreography and cheers. You said you love to dance, and so do I, and my mom is SO happy I'm actually in a school club. She's like freaking out happy. I don't want it to fizzle because I really don't want to let her down.

TOP SECRET: I can't be too excited around Wade, Braid, and Tape. You know how it is with them, but I am actually SO excited. So let's meet sometimes at lunch or after school to work on stuff. Kk? Let me know.

See you at rehearsal!

—Luna

I read the email over three times just in case it's some kind of prank or maybe she was hacked and this is from a fake email or something. But no, it's real! She actually wants to be an active part of the squad and come up with dances and cheers with me!

This is better than I could have ever expected.

"Why were you in the hall on your phone?" Mack asks me when I come back in.

"I just had to check something quick," I explain, and then take out my independent reading book, *Inside of a Dog*. Reading it is part of my mission to convince my parents to get a dog, but I have to get Mom back first. One thing at a time.

"You're being weird," Mack says. "You're up to something!"

I crack up. "Am not! Okay, reading now. Byeeee."

She rolls her eyes, but then laughs, too. "Whatever. Byeeeeee."

12

WHEN I GET TO THE gym after school for pep squad rehearsal, Mr. Woodson is sitting on the bleachers with a few of the other teachers. He has a clipboard and they're all huddled together and look very official, like I walked in on them discussing important business.

"Oh, sorry to interrupt," I say. "Wanted to just clear anything that would be in the way for pep squad practice." I'm actually not even sure if anyone besides Luna will show up, but either way I'm excited. A squad of two can still be peppy.

"No worries, Natty." He smiles. "Just give us a few moments."

I step outside and I don't plan on eavesdropping, but they're actually louder than they realize, I think.

"We'll have to strike," one of them says. "That's it.

These conditions are not workable. This life isn't sustainable. We don't have adequate supplies or training. Some days it doesn't even feel safe. We can't do this anymore!"

"This is why teachers need unions!" another teacher yells.

"Exactly!" someone else shouts, even louder than the one before.

Then one of them shushes the group and I can't hear anything for a few seconds.

"It's good we're at least a unified group," someone else adds.

"Agreed."

Everyone is silent then or maybe they're whispering, and soon Luna and Braid and the rest of them fall all over each other into the doorway, knocking into me a little.

"Lunch Girl, you're looking shady. Whatcha doing?" Tape asks me.

"Chillin'." I laugh, trying to break up the awkwardness of being clearly caught eavesdropping.

"In the doorway to the gym?" Braid scoffs. "Why are you the weirdest? You intrigue me."

I smile. "Does this mean you're here for the pep squad rehearsal or were you just randomly walking by?"

They all look at each other and explode into laughter.

"Nah, we're here for it." Wade shrugs.

"Yay!! I am so so so so happy you're all here!" I clap,

and then Tape tries to put a piece of duct tape on my face to get me to stop.

Wade adds, "I'm not planning to learn how to do any cheers or flips. I barely know how to clap."

We're still all sort of huddled in the doorway when I say, "Okay, everyone, hey!" I jump up and down, clapping my hands over my head. "Hey, Pep Squad! Hey, Pep Squad!"

"Great cheer, Natty!" Luna nudges me, like she's teasing in a friendly way. "Did you make that up?" Her eye makeup is smudgy and drippy, with one skinny black line going from her eyelashes to the side of her nose.

"I did! And that's just the beginning of it!" I lift my hand to high-five her. "I saw your email," I whisper in her ear. "And yes, I am so in."

I walk into the gym, and the rest of them follow me. The group of teachers who were with Mr. Woodson is gone by the time we get in there, and Mr. Woodson is sitting on the rusty folding chair he always sits on, writing some notes on his clipboard. He looks at me and I look at him and part of me thinks he knows I overheard them.

We all sit down on the bleachers, and I say, "Here's the thing. I'm not expecting you all to be, like, acrobatic gymnastics cheerleader people. We can make this what we want to make it! We are in control here!" I pause. "The routines will be manageable for us all to learn. I promise! Go, team."

The cutoff girls come in a few minutes later.

I'm kind of shocked that they're back, but I'm thrilled about it.

"Oh my god, this is definitely THE MOST HILARIOUS thing we've ever done," Kingsley says, intentionally loud, like she really wanted everyone in the gym to hear her.

"For real, the most hilarious," Rowan replies.

"Don't listen to them," Luna whispers to me. "They are *the worst ever, literally.*"

I smile and stand up to face the group. "Hi! Welcome! So happy you're back! We're just about to get started!" I yell out, all excited sounding. "We are going to learn a cheer today! Our first official cheer! And maybe a routine, too, if there's time! Get excited!"

Mr. Woodson looks up when I say this, like he's surprised or something.

"She is peppy, gotta give that to her," I hear Tape say to Wade, under her breath. I try to pretend like I didn't hear it, but I did hear it and it feels *amazing.*

"So let's start working on it!" I yell out, realizing that Mr. Woodson is really only focused on what he's doing, scribbling words on a lined yellow notepad, and not on the club at the moment. "Everybody up!" I lift my hands in the air. "Let's go! We'll do the cheer first."

They stand up slowly, not all at once.

"It starts: 'Hey, Pep Squad!' And then you all yell back, 'Hey!'"

They stare at me—blank faces on all of them.

"Ready to try?"

"Nope!" Tape yells back. "Not at all."

"Taaaape," Luna groans. "Come on. Just try. The tiniest bit of trying possible."

"Hey, Pep Squad!" I shout, bouncing from foot to foot and clapping.

"Hey," half say out loud, sort of sounding enthusiastic, and the other half go to sit down again.

I shake my head and laugh. "Getting better!"

"Natty," Mr. Woodson calls out from the other side of the bleachers. "I just got called into an emergency meeting. You okay here?"

I hesitate. It's sort of weird kids are allowed to just, like, be in a place without adult supervision. That would never happen at Willets. "Um, yeah, sure."

"Wonderful, thanks." He hustles off and he's almost out the door of the gym when he says, "Great job, team!"

"Yo, wait a minute." Braid sits up straight, realizing something important, it seems. "I just realized something. If we go all out for this pep squad or whatever, people will honestly be shocked. Like if we get out there and act all psyched about this place, it'll almost be the greatest prank ever. You hear me?"

"Um, what?" Tape continues drawing on her duct-tape armband with a fine-tip Sharpie.

"Everyone expects us to be haters," Braid says,

explaining. "So let's totally shock everyone."

"I know what you mean," Luna replies.

"Yeah! I like this. I really, really like this." I pump my arm in the air. "Whatever it takes to get into this! So, people, can we try this again?" I ask, starting to do a few jumping jacks. I keep expecting Running Kid to come in with his friends, but so far I don't see them. "Everyone up!"

They finally stand up again and follow my lead with the jumping jacks.

"Hey, Pep Squad!" I yell, almost out of breath.

"Hey!" They yell back, laughing and out of breath a little, too.

"Hey, Pep Squad!"

"Hey! Hey!"

"Hey, Pep Squad!"

"Hey! Hey! Hey!"

"Okay, so amazing job with that first part," I say. "And then the next part goes, 'We are Miller Creek! Miller Miller. Creek Creek Creek.' I say that part and then you guys say, 'Go, Frogs! Dance around! Go, Frogs!'" I pause. "Technically if we had a mascot, the mascot would come out then, but TBD on that. . . ."

I catch my breath and take a sip from my water bottle. "Sooo . . . Ready to try?"

"How long is this meeting?" Tape hisses to Braid and then Luna shoves her with her elbow.

We practice the cheer a few more times and then after that, I say, "So ready to see the routine I came up with? Remember it's just my first attempt, and I'm definitely open to suggestions."

"Just go, Lunch Girl!" Wade yells.

"Okay." I laugh, only the tiniest bit flustered. "Let me turn on the music."

I take my phone out of my pocket and turn the volume up as loud as it goes and I put on "Cheerleader."

"Why are we doing this song? I thought we're a pep squad, not, like, actual cheerleaders," Rowan calls out, putting her hair up in a high ponytail.

"It's just a great song!" I wave my arms sort of like a hula girl as the song starts, and then I do one leg kick to the side, then another leg kick to the other side. I demonstrate and watch their faces, and it just makes me laugh so hard that I have to stop in the middle to finish laughing and I almost fall over.

"Oh my god!" Rowan yells. "I have no idea what is going on here!"

"Okay, hang on, I—" I have to stop again because I literally cannot stop laughing. They all stare at me, but then they start laughing, too, and suddenly it's like no one can keep it together at all. We are all laughing, and I know it's not what we're supposed to be doing, and we're not working on the routine, but a whole group cracking up like this is just so good.

Finally, I say, "Okay, at this part, we all start running in a circle, one in front of the other, and then kick our legs in the middle as we run."

I show them the whole thing as slowly as possible.

"This choreography sucks!" Kingsley yells, tightening a pigtail. "Like, this is not even choreography. You're just, like, running? I think?" She laughs. "We can do so much more than this. Like for real. This is baaaaad." She stares at me. "Didn't you say you liked to dance?"

"Oh yeah, but more like dancing-around-the-kitchen-with-a-spatula-while-my-mom-makes-dinner kind of dancing." I crack up again.

"What is her deal?" Tape sneers. "Dancing with a spatula? What? I cannot figure her out!"

The cutoff girls start whispering to one another and then Terra shouts, "I'd be down to help with choreography, Natty. If you wanted some feedback . . ."

"Terra, what? You're going to actually, like, hang out with her?" Kingsley shrieks, louder than she'd intended, I think. "Stop it right now."

"Amazing, yes!" I shout. "I'd love your help!"

We have about five minutes left in the meeting, when we hear someone struggling to get in. We all turn to face the double doors of the gym.

"OMGEEEEE!" Tape yells. "Holy! I cannot. I just cannot." She covers her mouth in shock.

Everyone's mouths gape open as we watch a giant

frog waddling in through the door. Truly unable to walk, almost knocking into a folding chair and a stack of soccer goals.

"Um?" I say, running over to the frog. I inspect the costume for a minute, but then it hits me. I know who it is.

"Mack?"

"Yup. It's me. Sorry I'm late. I figured if I was gonna be a good friend and join this hellscape you created, I'd rather do it undercover."

I can't see her at all through the frog face, but I try to peek in through the little mesh mouth area, which is really where her eyes are.

"Sorry I didn't tell you earlier, but I wanted to surprise you," she continues.

"Mack! What? Are you serious? This is the BEST THING I HAVE EVER SEEN!" I'm screaming so loud and trying to hug her in this frog costume and I am just blown away that she found this and put it on and that she listened to me and she's willing to be the mascot. "Mack! I am blown away. Literally BLOWN AWAY."

"Calm down, Natty!" She says all forceful sounding, pulls the frog head off, and throws it a little. Her frizzy black hair is all disheveled. She tries to smooth it down and her cheeks turn pink. Mack turns away from me. "Someone was giving it away in the Miller Creek Buy Nothing Group online. I was searching for a suit for my dad to wear to a job interview and I saw it. A leftover

Halloween costume or whatever. Why do you always have to make everything so intense?"

She picks up the frog head and storms out of the gym.

"Can everyone hang on a second? I'll be back."

They all grumble and go back to the bleachers, pulling out their phones. I find Mack in the girls' locker room.

"Mack, sorry, I just got so excited. This is amazing and I want to hear about it all."

"Fine, you will, just not in front of all of *them*." She nudges her head toward the locker room door. "Don't make everything such a scene all the time."

"Got it. Okay. I understand."

She looks down at the ground and then back up at me, sideways smiling. "You like it, though?"

"Um, like it? I'm obsessed! And the fact that you did it and then surprised me . . . I mean, Mack." I stop myself. "Okay, I'm chill. It's great. Come out when you're ready. We have only a few minutes left."

"Okay." She full smiles, which for Mack is pretty much like ten smiles combined. She's not a big smiler.

I walk back to the gym, and everyone is slumped over each other on the bleachers. Braid's head is resting on Wade's shoulder, and the cutoff girls are huddled together like they're about to fall asleep.

"Okay, everyone, thanks so much for all the energy today. I think we're done for the day. See you guys Monday for the next event." I pause, deflated a little that

Running Kid didn't show up like he said he would. "Oh, it's actually for boys soccer, not cross-country, obvs, that was the other day. Sorry about the mix-up."

"What? No!" Rowan says. "Brian Wells is on that team and I'm in love with him and we are sooooo not ready. We can't, like, perform for people and do that routine! He can't see me doing that running thing!"

I ignore her negativity and the fact that she just told the whole squad about her crush. "It'll be awesome. We'll go with the flow. Don't worry. It doesn't have to be perfect." I pause. "You know what Taylor Swift said. 'I think fearless is having fears but jumping anyway.'"

I nod, letting that sink in for them, but they just stare at me.

"Don't worry!" I do one final leg kick. "It's all gonna be awesome!"

"You think everything is awesome," Braid adds. "It's most definitely not."

"Anyway, have a fabulous rest of your afternoon." I smile. "Sign the sign-in sheet on the clipboard so you all get credit for being here; write down your names and emails please, for real this time!"

They all grumble to each other that this is ridiculous and it's not fair how I'm forcing them to perform when they're not ready. I ignore it. We'll be ready. We'll figure it out. Sometimes in life you need to make stuff up as you go.

On their way out of the gym, I hear Tape say to the rest

of them, "I have no idea how we got ourselves into this. I really hate her."

I stand there frozen for a few minutes, those words echoing behind my eyeballs. A few tears trickle out, but I wipe them away with the bottom of my T-shirt. No one's here, so I don't feel weird about the sliver of my stomach showing.

Saying you hate someone is so common now, it doesn't even have any meaning at all.

I open my eyes and Mack's right there, holding the frog head, still wearing the bottom part of the costume. I have no idea how long she's been here.

"Oh hey! Um, yeah, so want to walk home?" I smile and clear my throat. "Today was really great."

She looks at me wide-eyed. "Natty, you okay?"

"Yeah. I'm great! Why?" I throw my backpack onto my shoulders and take a long sip from my water bottle.

"Natty! Loser Theresa just said she hates you. . . . How are you great? You don't look great . . . at all. . . ."

"I'm totally fine. Honestly." I laugh. "So what? One person says she hates me. I can take it. Plenty of people hate plenty of people." I shrug. "Come on, let's go. I want to get one of those coffee milkshakes at the donut place on the way home."

"That does sound good. I need to change out of this, though, and put it in my locker. I'll be back."

Sniffling, I walk over to the padded wall, lean my

forehead against it, and close my eyes.

The tears come flooding back, but I blink as hard as I can and quickly wipe away the droplets with my hand.

It's fine. Everything's fine. This is not at all like what happened with The Core in Willets. Mack found a mascot costume and she actually wants to *be* the mascot! The rehearsal was actually great today and Luna and Terra want to help with choreography and so what that my first routine was bad? It can only go up from here!

Everything is good. It's great, actually.

I just don't know why I can't stop crying. I squeeze my eyes tight to prevent any more tears from leaking out.

Mack comes back, and she says, "Natty . . . you're not okay. . . ."

"A bug just flew into my eye! Out of nowhere. Does it look really red?"

"Yeah, right." She rolls her eyes. "A little red, not too bad. . . ."

We walk quietly out of school and Mack says, "I don't get it. Why can't you just admit you're upset?"

"Mack! I'm not upset! Oh my goodness!" I start laughing. "I am totally fine!"

She shakes her head. "Okay, Natty. Whatever you say."

13

ON SATURDAY MORNING, I WAKE up to the sound of my phone vibrating next to my bed in the attic. At first I think it's Gracie, since she's the only one who texts me, but then I see that it's a group text, with Luna and Terra!

My first group text in Miller Creek! This feels like a big moment! A *shehecheyanu* moment, as my mom calls them. The *shehecheyanu* is the prayer Jews say to mark special and new occasions.

Luna: Natty! I ran into Terra when I was out with my dad picking up groceries this morning. We totally bonded by the strawberries about the pep squad LOL.

Luna: Wanna meet up to make up some routines today? We're both free!

Luna: and that routine defffff needs work lol

Terra: I'm in. obviously!

Me: YES! OFC! I AM SO EXCITED!

Luna: okay but stop typing in all caps

Me: hahaha kk

Terra: where and when?

Me: my backyard, 11:30?

I drop a pin to show them where my grandparents' house is, shower quickly, and run downstairs to tell everyone I have friends coming over.

While waiting for Luna and Terra on the front steps and finishing a piece of Grandma's s'mores pie (not the most nutritious breakfast but it's all I had time for), I hear someone calling my name.

I look up, and my heart sinks.

It's Mack.

Luna and Terra will be here in five minutes. I don't know what the deal is with all of them, but I have a feeling Mack won't be thrilled the three of us are hanging outside of school on a weekend.

"What's up?" she asks. "Waiting for another Little League game to start?"

I laugh. "No, but good call—when is the next one? Maybe we can try out some of our routines there?"

I have no idea why I'm having a conversation with her when I need her to not be here in five minutes.

"Um, no." She sits down on the step next to me and my heart pounds. How am I going to get her to leave? She can't be here when they come; everyone will be all weird around each other.

"Are you eating pie at, like, eleven in the morning?" she asks me.

I laugh and look down at my plate. "Uh, yeah, but it's s'mores pie so, like, graham crackers. That's kind of breakfast-y, right?"

"Not at all. . . ." She rolls her eyes. "But it looks good."

"I'd offer you some, but this is the last slice. Next time for sure, k?"

She nods. "Aren't you going to ask why I'm out wandering by myself on a Saturday morning?"

"Oh, um, yeah, sorry, got lost in my thoughts for a second." I take my phone out to see if Luna and Terra texted, praying that they're running late for some reason. But no, nothing. I expect to hear their footsteps coming up the street at any minute. "Why are you out wandering by yourself on a Saturday morning?"

"Because my house sucks right now; my parents always fight the most on the weekend."

"People fight because they care," I say. "Like, it's actually worse if they don't fight."

"What?" she asks, annoyed sounding, like I'm speaking in a made-up language.

"No, I'm serious, if they didn't care or want things to be better, they'd just be quiet and, like, not even talk to each other," I explain. "It's good that they're fighting."

She shuffles her feet against the pavement. "That's super dumb, Natty."

"It's true." I shrug. "And also, like, maybe moving will actually be really good, a change of scenery and stuff, a chance at a fresh start." I smile. "Honestly, just try to think positively, and it'll all be okay."

She stares at me for a moment and then starts ranting about how it's horrible and why can't I even see reality and I'm trying to listen and be a good friend but I'm too nervous about when Luna and Terra will get here—it's my first official plan with friends here outside of school, and it needs to be good.

Mack stops talking in the middle of her rant because she hears something, and then she gets up to look down the street to see what it is.

Oh no oh no oh no.

She says, "Lilian and Terra are about to walk by. Don't look. It's like the sun. You can't stare directly at them."

Oh no oh no oh no.

"Actually, they're—"

"Heeyyyyyy," Terra sings, interrupting me, as she strolls up the cement path to the house. "Heeeyyyyy girl hee—" But she stops in the middle when she sees Mack.

"Ummmm." Luna rolls her lips together. "Didn't know she was joining us."

"Ummmmm yeah," Mack says. "I'll be leaving now."

She huffs as she gets up from the step and then

whispers, "Thanks for being the worst." She runs down the path and keeps running until we can't see her anymore.

"What was that about?" Luna asks.

"She was walking by, and she saw me outside, and she stopped to chat, and I didn't have a chance to explain that you were coming over to practice."

"I don't even get why she hates everyone," Terra says. "She could've stayed."

"No, thanks," Luna replies. "I can handle only so much in one day. . . ."

"Huh?" Terra looks at her a little crooked. "What's that supposed to mean?"

"Okay, everyone." I put a hand on each of their shoulders. "Let's chill. We're gonna come up with an awesome routine, and I'm so excited. What a blessing that you ran into each other today!"

"A blessing?" Terra scrunches up her nose.

"Yes. Come on. Backyard. Now."

"I just feel like the energy is off now," Luna says when we get to the backyard, slumping down on a patio chair. "I can't shake Mack's downer vibes."

"The energy is not off!" I clap and start bouncing from foot to foot. "The energy is what we make it to be! We can bring the good vibes! We *are* the good vibes!"

"What are you even saying?" Terra asks, lying down

on one of the lounges. "You're like a motivational speaker windup doll or something!"

"She so is! I keep saying that!" Luna says, completely cracking up, and a second later Terra does, too, and soon all three of us are laughing, like nothing in the world has ever been funnier.

"Okay, let's just start, for real," I say, when we finally stop laughing. "I want a routine that goes well with 'Cheerleader,' because it's *impossible* not to feel fired up when that song is playing. I mean, just singing it at the cross-country meet felt amazing!"

"If you say so." Luna shrugs. "JK, I agree with you, for real."

Terra nods. "So yeah, I agree. I love that song, too, but here's the thing," she says, pulling up her wide-leg capri jeans and then putting her hands on her hips. "We can't make the choreography too complicated, or people will just not be able to do it."

Luna nods. "She's right."

I smile, feeling like something magical is about to happen right now. "Go on."

"And remember, whatever we do, we'll do it all in sync, so if one person messes up, the whole thing doesn't look as good," Terra explains.

"Right," I reply. "Exactly! A fully united squad! Woo! Okay, I'm putting on the song!"

We listen three times through, and then we start coming up with the routine.

"Okay, first idea!" Luna bursts up from the patio chair. "The song starts and we do a kind of marching in sync thing. Oh, let's air trumpet out!"

"Oooh yes, brilliant, Lil— Luna." Terra corrects herself. "Oops, sorry. I still think of you as Lilian."

"It's okay. Luna's still a pretty new thing, started in sixth grade." She soft-smiles. "Okay, so yeah, we do the air trumpet out." She pauses to think. "Then windmill over our heads, both directions. Windmill right, windmill left."

"Yes! Fierce!" Terra starts doing the whole routine slowly so we can see it. "And then step and clap, step and clap, for like eight beats." She demonstrates. "Arm up and then across our body, point to the floor! Arm up other side and across our body, point to the floor!"

"Yes! I love this SO much! Yes!" I scream.

"OMG, this is amazing and not even that hard!" Luna yells, pausing the song. "My people literally cannot dance *at all* so we need to make it eaaaasssyyyy."

I start laughing again because Luna has such a silly way of speaking sometimes, but the truth is, I never see her having this much fun at school. She's like a different version of herself right now, in my backyard, making up dance moves with Terra and me.

"Right," Terra says, turning the music back on. "Then

we do hands out, palms up, on our sides, like the emoji"—
she laughs—"and when it says 'do you think I'm pretty'
we sort of do a hand gesture like displaying our faces.
And for the 'no, not really' we shake our fingers!"

"Yes!" I scream. "Ah-mazing!!"

"And when the chorus comes back on, we do side step,
clap, side step, clap, box step, and windmill, point and
across, point and across," Luna explains.

The song ends and Luna says, "Oh emmm geee, first
of all that was ah-may-zing. And second of all, Terra, do
you remember that dance we had to do in second grade,
when that square dance troupe came and we, like, had
to do an introductory welcome dance for them? Am I
remembering this correctly?"

I feel so intrigued, hearing these stories about them
as little kids. I came in late to the whole social dynamic
here, but I want to know everything about the way it used
to be, and how things got to be the way they are now.

Terra's eyes get really wide. "Yes! You are so right, it
was like a big deal. We had to practice for weeks, and
for some reason our class was picked to do the dance.
Remember how Mrs. Tarellick would get so frustrated
with us?"

"Oh! And that kid Nick Patello refused to do it, and he
just sat on the side of the stage in a folding chair?" Luna
erupts into laughter. "What happened to him?"

"I think he moved," Terra says quietly, like a very

distant memory is resurfacing in her brain. "Wow, I have not thought about this in *so long*."

"Me neither." Luna shakes her head. "Super weird to remember the dumb stuff we used to do."

"Totally," Terra replies, and I start to feel left out but not in the worst way, just sort of like I'm watching a show instead of performing in it. "Okay, so, Natty, put the song on again and watch Luna and me do it, and then tell us what you think."

"K! Yay! I am so excited!"

I put the song on again and they start doing the routine: air trumpet out, windmill, pointing up and across, the side steps and claps, emoji hands, face display, finger shake, box step. It already looks so good, it's hard to believe they literally just came up with it.

"Wow! That looked absolutely, positively AH-MAZ-ING!" I scream.

"We're pretty awesome," Luna says with a little curtsy.

"Some might even say dynamic duo." Terra smiles, and then Luna lifts her eyebrows, like that's some relic of a private joke from a really, really long time ago.

We end up doing the routine three more times, all together, and by the end of the third time, I feel like I've mastered it. After that, the three of us sit on my patio and Grandma brings us out a pitcher of her peach lemonade and some pretzels with French onion dip in a little bowl on the side. And we stay outside chatting and discussing the routine, and old private jokes between Luna and Terra pop up every few minutes.

And sometimes they explain them and sometimes they don't, but with each passing moment, it feels like today is a turning point.

"Wait, I just had a brilliant idea," Terra says. "We should be the captains of the squad, you know how that's like a thing?"

I nod.

This is happening. This is really happening. They're getting into my idea, and they want us to actually *be* something. Together.

"Um, wow, way to be the most enthusiastic person EVER!" Luna shouts, and then cracks up. "But yes, I do know what you mean, and yes it's brilliant, and my mom will literally flip that I'm actually in charge of a school-related thing!"

"Yes!" I laugh. "Love this, love all of this. And maybe our squad can even get so good, we can enter competitions and stuff. Some are even at Disney World, I think." My skin prickles when I think about all the possibilities.

"Wait, how's the squad gonna learn this before Monday's game, though?" Terra asks, biting her bottom lip.

"We'll teach it to them really quickly," Luna says. "Like right before."

"It's gonna be sooo bad, though, if no one really knows it." Terra frowns. "There won't be time."

"No, stop." I shake my head. "It'll be great! We'll do our best! GOOD VIBES ONLY, PEOPLE!"

"Oh, here she goes again," Luna mocks, and we all crack up. "Motivational Speaker Natty Blaken."

Luna and Terra stay for a little while longer, and we keep coming up with ideas: maybe a bake sale to fund-raise for uniforms, strategies to get the other members of the squad as excited as we are. We have a whole plan to put up flyers around town for the pep rally and I'm even going to email the mayor and ask him to come kick off the event!

After they leave, I sit on the deck and soak in what's left of the afternoon sun. The birds are chirping; there's a perfect little breeze. I actually had friends over today! We hung out and laughed and snacked and came up with a whole awesome routine!

It's because *good vibes only* is the way to go; no doubt about it. We didn't let ourselves get sucked into Mack's downer energy and everything was amazing.

From: Natty Blaken
To: Mayor Gerald Giff
Subject: MILLER CREEK JUNIOR HIGH PEP RALLY

Dear Mayor Giff:

Hi! I'm Natty Blaken, a seventh grader, new to Miller Creek, even though my dad grew up here. I started a pep squad at Miller Creek Junior High and we're having our first ever pep rally the second Monday in October! I'd love it if you could come and make some opening remarks. I know you're very busy, but please get back to me when you can and I'll give you all the details. Feel free to call when you have a moment: 516-555-2222.

Best wishes,
Natty J. Blaken

Mack isn't on the bus this morning, and when I text her to ask if we should wait, I don't get any reply. I bet she's still soaking in all the negative vibes from Saturday, and I probably should have checked in yesterday. I'm sure she's upset that I was hanging out with Terra and Luna, but it's not my fault, and she shouldn't be mad about it!

When I get off the bus and walk into school, the cutoff girls are hanging out by the main entrance like one of them forgot their homework, maybe, and they're waiting for a parent to bring it to them. I'm not sure that's what's happening; it's just a hunch I have.

Terra waves to me, and I wave back.

I walk toward my locker and overhear some of their conversation.

"I mean, it started out as this thing we could do, and, like, make fun of her. . . . How did it get to the point that we're actually participating and you're, like, in charge of choreography, Ter? And hanging out with her outside of school?" It's Kingsley. She has the squeakiest voice of all of them.

"No clue. But I'm excited about it, actually!" Terra pauses. "It was fun to hang out with her." She pauses. "And also, like, the whole school will see us perform, and that'll be cool and just, like, I don't know, fun!"

"Ter, you just said 'fun' a million times," Kingsley says like it's the worst thing in the world. "But whatever. Ro and I can still make fun of her and, like, torture her life a little bit . . . and be in the pep squad and get community service at the same time."

"Kingsie, stop," Rowan adds. "Seriously."

Wow. Okay. Let Kingsley try and torture my life—I don't even know what that means, but also, it's literally impossible. Plus Rowan doesn't seem to feel that way, and Terra definitely doesn't.

I walk on, my head held high, and when I reach my locker, Mack is there, lying on the floor, resting her head on her backpack, doodling in her little notebook.

"Mack!" I yelp. "You're here already?"

She lifts her head up slowly. "No . . . I'm an illusion of myself. . . ." She wiggles her fingers in the air in front of her to seem all spooky or something.

"Okay, but why weren't you on the bus? And you didn't respond to my text." I hang up my jean jacket and grab a few textbooks from the top shelf. "Are you okay?"

She sits up. "Well, first of all, I still hate you for hanging out with those people and not telling me, but also, nope. I AM NOT OKAY. We literally moved in the middle of the night. I think my dad thought we'd escape paying the last month's rent that way. He loaded a U-Haul himself and some buddy of his brought a truck for our other furniture, and we got to this dumpster condo at like three in the morning." She looks up at me. "Guess we'll never ride the bus together again."

"Whoa, Mack. That's like a literal out-of-a-movie adventure!"

"That is not how I'd describe it, Natty. Not at all. . . ."

"It's gonna be great when you're all settled in the new place, though. I know you say it's a dumpster, but with your eye for design and artistic ability—you will make it look soooo amazing. For real." I pause. "It's honestly going to be better than you could have ever imagined."

"Um, no, Natty, not one bit. Please let's just stop talking. I need to rest before the day starts, k?"

"K."

Mack closes her eyes and then she falls asleep on the floor for another five minutes before the bell rings. Actual deep sleep, snoring and everything, and I have to gently tap her shoulder because even the loud ding and everyone shuffling in the hallway don't wake her up.

"Advisory, come on," I say softly. "Let's go." I reach out my hands to help her up and she groans and smooths out the sides of her hair. I grab her backpack from the floor and even put it on her shoulders, and then she follows behind me as we walk to Ms. Lamlot's classroom.

"You'll feel awake soon," I tell her. "By the time we get to the soccer game, you'll be so energized and pumped up. The adrenaline alone will carry you all the way through. It's kind of amazing how adrenaline works."

"Stop saying adrenaline," Mack groans.

When we get to Advisory, I feel like I actually *am* seeing an illusion because my dad is standing at the doorway, talking to Ms. Lamlot.

"Dad?" I stammer. "What are you doing here?"

"Oh, uh, Natty. You left this on the table." He hands me a slip of paper that he signed, authorizing me to be allowed to participate in after-school activities.

My eyebrows crinkle. "Oh, um, I don't need that. You already signed it, and I turned it in, and then brought it home and forgot to recycle it. . . . See the teacher's signature at the bottom?" I show him Mr. Woodson's scrawly handwriting.

"Oops, sorry." He shrugs and moves his weight to the other foot. "I thought it was important."

Ms. Lamlot stares at him and then starts laughing. And then he starts laughing with her, and nudges her arm a little, and I don't totally know what's happening.

"Uh, thanks, though." I smile. "Guess I'll head into class. . . ."

My dad laughs again, but it feels like I'm not in on the joke somehow. "Have a great day, Natty. Love you."

I walk in and sit down and then crane my neck a little to see the doorway because my dad and Ms. Lamlot are still standing there, chatting.

Advisory should've started two minutes ago.

"Wait, that's your dad?" Mack leans her head over and

whispers a second after I sit down.

I nod, still trying to see what's actually happening in the doorway.

"Way to tell me he is going out with Ms. Lamlot," she says, doodling some kind of very intricate robot in her notebook.

I burst out laughing. "What? Mack! No way. They know each other from high school."

"Um, way, Natty." She eye-bulges. "What planet do you live on?"

"Earth," I reply, like it's obvious because obviously it's obvious, but then I feel really dumb for saying that.

We stop talking and Ms. Lamlot pops her head into the classroom and tells us that we're delayed because we are waiting on some kind of supply delivery and that we should just catch up on homework or read or draw or meditate . . . any of the above.

"Nice of you to not ask me anything else about my shady, middle-of-the-night move from hell, Natty," Mack says, still doodling in her notebook, not looking over at me. "Nice of you to care at all. I guess I shouldn't be surprised, but still."

"I do care, I really do. I wasn't sure if you wanted to really talk that much about it," I say, turning sideways to face her.

"Uh-huh. Yeah, right." She rolls her eyes. "Saying you weren't sure if I wanted to talk about it is the EASY WAY

OUT, Natty." She says the last part all forceful and then turns away from me.

I look over at her notebook and her doodles are seriously incredible. I want to put her in charge of the posters for pep squad, but my whole read-a-room thing tells me this isn't the time to bring that up.

Finally, Ms. Lamlot comes in with a stack of notebooks.

"Students. So sorry for the delay here." She sits down at her desk and clasps her hands against her chest the way she always does and closes her eyes and then waits for a few moments before speaking.

"That's gonna be your new mom," Mack whispers.

"Oh my god!" I laugh. "Stop!"

The weird thing is Ms. Lamlot's style and vibe are sort of similar to my mom's. Maybe that's why I find her so comforting.

"So, students. I reached out to our administration to purchase a meditation notebook for all of you. . . . They weren't able to come through, but I found some amazing things at the dollar store. . . ." She rolls her lips together. "I know finances can be tight and it's hard to purchase extra supplies. So please take care of these journals. They will be a lifeline for your meditation. We will work in them every morning, but please feel free to use them at other times of the day as well, anytime you meditate."

She looks out at the class, and our eyes meet for a second and she smiles at me in her chamomile-tea way and I smile back. She's so different from everyone else in Miller Creek. I wonder if she realizes that.

"Natty, want to come help me pass these out?"

I nod and hop up from my chair. "I'd love to!"

"That girl is soooo weird," someone in the back yells, and then another kid shushes that person.

"Oh, Natty," Mack says, after I'm done passing out the notebooks and back at my desk. "Do you realize it sucks here yet?"

"Nope. Not at all." I smile. "I love it here!"

She throws a pencil at my head, and I duck and miss it.

"Mack, please." Ms. Lamlot shakes her head. "We are supposed to be meditating. Not throwing pencils. We're never supposed to be throwing pencils. Let's center ourselves."

She closes her eyes and bows her head.

"Let's center ourselves," she repeats.

15

WHEN I CHECK MY PHONE after school, I see that I have a string of texts from Gracie. She seems to do this kind of a lot lately.

Gracie: omg so much drama to discuss with you

Gracie: you won't even believe it

Gracie: sooo upset rn

Me: Gracie! You're amazing & everything's gonna be fine!

Me: don't get sucked into the drama!

Me: gg but will text more later!

Gracie: Nattyyyyyyy!! I miss you sooo much.

Me: I looooove you.

Gracie: xoxoxoxoxo

Me: XOXOXOXOXOXO

Gracie's text about whatever drama is going on nags at me a little, and so does the conversation with Mack earlier when she said I didn't care that much about her move, plus the thing she brought up about Ms. Lamlot and my dad. But I can't deal with any of that now.

I have twenty minutes before the game and I need to remind the squad to meet in the gym! I run to the main office to see if I can make a quick announcement.

"Hiii," I say out of breath to Sheila. "I need to make one quick announcement for the pep squad, about our event today—the boys soccer game—and I'd just like to—"

"Go right ahead, dear." Sheila slides the microphone across the desk again. "I don't need all the details."

She goes back to her magazine, doing that thing where she licks her finger to turn the pages.

"Hi, Miller Creek Junior High! It's Natty. Just wanted to make an announcement for the pep squad—please meet in the gym, um, right now! Just a quick little catch-up before the game. And yeah, see you soon! K, bye!"

My heart races as I sprint down the hallway, secretly hoping that Running Kid hears my announcement and actually comes to the meeting today. I walk through the double doors to the gym, and the lunch table crew members are the only ones there.

They're all slumped over against the padded walls, sleeping and drawing on each other's arms.

"Natty!" Luna says. "See how good we're doing? We're here early!"

"Very good, Luna." I smile. "A plus."

"Wait, do we get graded for this for real?" Tape asks. "I had no clue."

"Taaaaaape, we don't get graded. It's an expression," Wade replies. He shakes his head. "These people, Natty. Am I right?"

I shrug. "It's all good. Actually. It's all GREAT!" I jump up and down and clap my hands above my head. "Everyone up! Come on! Up on your feet."

Luna jumps up first and runs over to me, and we link arms.

"Rock Star Captain," I whisper to her.

"Okay, everyone, quick warm-up and then I have a very important announcement to make," I say, grabbing my phone out of my jeans pocket and putting on my Pep Squad playlist.

Slowly they all get up, looking sluggish, and basically just snapping their fingers.

But I keep jumping up and down and dancing and then a minute later the cutoff girls traipse in.

"Hii," I say. "Come join!"

"Ew," Kingsley replies. "I can't with this."

"Just go with it," Rowan adds.

Terra runs over and links arms with me. "I'm actually

really excited about this," she whispers.

Then we start doing a kick-line kind of thing, and at first we stay together, but then I do one kick out of place and start laughing, and we all almost fall over.

A minute later, Mack comes in, wearing her awesome frog costume, and everyone cracks up. I swear they're into it. Right behind her is Running Kid. At first I think my eyes are playing tricks on me, but he's actually coming into the gym right now.

"Hey, uh, sorry we're late, but . . . I brought some friends with me!"

My stomach gets all flip-floppy.

"Yay! Welcome!" I clap. "Quick! Tell me your names."

"I'm Lance," he says. "That's Marcus, Trey, and Chris." He points at each of them. Okay, I don't have time to come up with ways to remember them now; that'll have to wait.

"K, we're all learning a new routine today," I tell them, my voice catching in my throat. "So just follow along, and we'll do the best we can."

"Shouldn't we be wearing school colors or something?" Kingsley sing-songs.

"Yes! Definitely for next time." I pause, trying to catch my breath, too. "Did everyone hear Kingsley's amazing idea?"

Most of them just stare at me blankly, some groan.

I say, "For the next event, everyone come in green and gray, Miller Creek colors!"

"She said I had an amazing idea!" Kingsley smiles, looking around the gym to make sure everyone acknowledges her.

Well, that feels like progress. Clearly a compliment goes a long way.

"So, Terra and Luna, wanna help teach the new routine?" I say.

"No running in a circle today, Lunch Girl?" Tape smiles and lifts her eyebrows. I might be making this up, but I think her tone has softened a little.

I put on the song, and they do the whole thing: the air trumpet, windmill, pointing up and across, the side steps and claps, emoji hands, face display, shaking their fingers, and the box step. It's like they've known this routine their whole entire lives!

"Okay, wow." Rowan eye-bulges, playing with a strand of her hair. "I gotta admit. That was good."

"Really good!" Kingsley echoes. "Go, Terra! Go, Terra!"

"Yeah, it was good but there's no way I'm gonna remember that with like three seconds to learn it," Braid says. "Like zero point zero chance."

"Gotta agree there," Lance adds. "We'll try but . . ."

"It's fine! Just follow along! Luna, Terra, and I will be up at the front." I clap. "So, yeah, we gotta go!"

"We didn't even practice it one time, Lunch Girl!" Wade yells. "This is ludicrous!"

"It'll be great, don't worry!"

We make it out to the soccer field before the players take the field and there's actually a pretty good crowd. People brought beach chairs and stuff and some are sitting on blankets on the grass. I expected bleachers by the soccer field, but there aren't any.

I don't see Mr. Woodson anywhere and I start to worry he forgot about the game.

I get everyone to huddle up and Wade says, "Uh, even the teacher bailed on this." He flips his faded baseball cap from back to front. "Not a great sign, Lunch Girl. Off to a tremulous start . . ."

"It's all good, Wade. Mr. Woodson is coming." I stretch my arms above my head from side to side. "Come on, let's go. This is our time. We'll do the cheer first and then the routine, and then we'll all chill on the grass and cheer throughout the game! We are going to be absolutely, positively GREAT!"

I don't see a megaphone or speaker or even a microphone even though I'd asked Mr. Woodson to get those for me. It doesn't matter. I have a loud voice.

"Hey, Miller Creek!" I shout to the crowd. "I said . . . HEY, MILLER CREEK!"

Finally the crowd catches on and they shout back a loud "HEY!"

126

I turn around and face the squad now. They're all looking in different directions, staring off into the distance,
weight resting on one foot instead of on both like they're
ready to begin.

"Hey, Pep Squad!" I yell.

I motion for them to perk up, get excited, and finally
they do.

"Hey!" they yell back, all at once, and it sounds good.
They actually sound excited.

We do this back and forth a few times, adding another
"hey" like we always do. We all hustle off to the side a bit
and I motion for Luna and Terra to come to the front of
the line with me, so we can lead the group.

It feels like the most amazing kind of relief to have
them there, like the moment ibuprofen kicks in and your
cramps are finally fading away.

"This is gonna be so bad," Terra hisses. "I wish we had
more time to practice the new routine."

"It's okay," I whisper. "We'll do the best we can; think
of it more as freestyle vibes."

"This is hilarious," Luna says.

"Thank you for being up here with me," I say softly to
both of them.

Luna replies, "It'll be a hot mess. But we can only go
up from here."

I turn on the song and we air trumpet out. My heart
is pounding so hard and fast and somehow feels like it's

louder than the speaker.

"Natty, we don't know this AT ALL," Kingsley sing-songs loud enough for the whole squad to hear.

"Sssh, it's okay, just go with it," I reply.

We *are* a hot mess. None of us are coordinated or doing any of the moves together. Half of the squad forgets the windmill, and we're definitely not all stepping and clapping in the same direction. Some of the claps aren't even on beat.

Shockingly, the crowd doesn't seem to mind! They're clapping with us, and some people are singing. This song is actual magic somehow. Everyone is smiling!

Then right as the song ends, I peek around to the side and nod at Mack in the frog costume so she knows it's her time.

I yell as loud as I can, "Give it up for the new Miller Creek mascot! Freddy the Frog!"

Everyone in the crowd starts cheering then—louder and more excited and so surprised seeming.

My whole body feels warm and energized like I could sprint around the field ten times without even stopping.

"Go, Freddy! Go, Freddy!" I yell as Mack dances around in the costume. I motion for the rest of the squad to join in the cheer with me. We all yell, "Go Freddy!" at the same time, and I swear the entire crowd looks blown away. Like they've never, ever seen this level of enthusiasm in their entire lives.

"We are Miller Creek! Miller Miller. Creek Creek Creek!" I shout, starting our cheer again.

And then the squad actually shouts in unison, "Go, Frogs! Dance around! Go, Frogs!"

It's a miracle, and the squad is dancing, too! So maybe the routine was a mess, but our cheer was perfect! Both times!

"Welllll," I say, loud and proud to everyone in the crowd. "Now that we're all fired up and ready to rock, let's cheer for our aaaaammmaaaaazzzzzing Miller Creek Junior High boys soccer team!" I pump my hands in the air, and everyone cheers and then I walk off to the side, and the rest of the squad follows behind me.

"Guys," I say, a little out of breath, gesturing for the squad to come in close for a huddle. "That was literally amazing. It was our first event, and we got people excited, and I think that was our main goal and we succeeded with that."

"Who is this girl?" Kingsley loud-whispers to Rowan. "She's, like, too excited to even make fun of anymore."

I ignore that and pretend I didn't hear it. But truthfully, it's an amazing compliment.

"Um, Lunch Girl, pretty sure we totally sucked and can't dance *at all*. And since Woodson didn't even show, can you please tell him we tried? So we get the credit or whatever. . . . Don't wanna be doing this for the rest of my life." Tape adjusts the duct tape on her elbows and looks around at the rest of lunch table crew. "Wait, are we in this all year?"

They shrug.

"Natty, I feel like that was a really good first try, with our fab new routine," Luna jumps in. "Honestly. Ignore the haters. The cheer was so good!"

"She's right! For real, I'm fired up. This squad is going to be so good when we get it together," Terra says, all enthusiastic.

"Ew, what is happening?" Kingsley squishes up her face. "Does Ter remember when Lilian puked while running through the sprinkler at her house in third grade?"

Luna's face flashes bright red at that point and Terra looks at the grass.

"Yeah! People! Yeah!" Lance screams, and starts running in place. "That was fire! Like actual fire somehow because I think I might have some thigh chafing, but wow!" He turns to his friends. "Right?"

"It was excellent," Marcus replies.

"I agree! You all CRUSHED IT!" I smile, resisting the urge to hug Lance. "So yeah, let's go sit on the side and cheer on the team from there for the rest of the event. Way to go, all of you! Don't forget weekly rehearsal tomorrow!"

"One thing at a time, Lunch Girl," Braid says. "I'm beat from today."

"Right." I smile. "One thing at a time."

We start walking to the side of the field and I say, "Wait, one more thing."

They all groan.

"Can we please give a round of applause to Freddy the Frog? The best mascot in the history of mascots!" I clap. "Freddy is the best! Freddy is the best!" I cheer.

"Okay, thanks, but also, stop and never do that again," Mack says, her words coming out muffled through Freddy's frog head. "I need to change out of this. I'm sweating in places I didn't know I could sweat."

"Ew. Seriously gross." Tape shakes her head.

I sit down on the grass, stretch out my legs and exhale the deepest exhale of my life, I think.

Little by little, this squad is coming together. There's no denying it.

16

MACK CHANGES OUT OF HER costume, and then we hang out a little on the grass and do homework. It's such a nice day and she doesn't want to go back to her "dumpster condo" anyway. I guess she's gotten over being mad at me for hanging out with Luna and Terra on Saturday, because she's choosing to be here with me right now. I'm glad to be outside longer, and also medium concerned about Mr. Woodson. He never came, and I'm kind of hoping he'll find his way out here and explain. I hope he's okay.

"Saw your dad with Ms. Lamlot again, when I was coming into school," Mack says. "Parent-teacher conference that my parents didn't know about, or they just hang out?"

I shrug. "No clue. He knows like one person in this

town, and that's her."

"I thought he grew up here? Shouldn't he know lots of people?" she asks, putting the social studies worksheet in her folder.

"Well, you'd think, but also he hated growing up here, and he was so excited to leave, and he kind of made sure everyone knew he hated it. . . ." My voice trails off as I stare at the trees in the distance.

"Mmm-hmm." Mack seems to zone out for a second.

"That's why I feel like a negative attitude can really just make things so much worse. Like, if my dad had tried to act positive or at least not like he hated everything about Miller Creek when he lived here, he might have more friends, and he might be happier now." I tuck some hair behind my ear. "See what I mean?"

"I guess, but that's so super fake. He hated it. What was the point of pretending he didn't? I hate fake stuff." She pulls out her notebook and starts writing her English essay on *The Outsiders*.

"It's not fake. It's your perspective. It's all about how you see stuff, and the vibes you want to put out." I finish my last math problem and put everything away, even my pencil case. Completing homework for the day is always the best feeling. And it's like you know you'll have more tomorrow, but in that moment, you're done and it seems like you should throw a teeny, tiny party for yourself.

"Whatever, Natty and your stupid 'good vibes only'

perspective." She looks me right in the eyes, like she's staring directly into my soul. "You can't even see that your dad is hanging out with our teacher, and your whole plan to get your mom here is failing."

I ignore her completely. There is absolutely no way she's right about any of that. "Wait, how far is um, *dumpster condo*—I hate to call it that—from here? Can I walk you home?"

She looks surprised that I've asked, and it takes her a few seconds to respond. "It's close. It's like school is in the middle of our homes now, so it could be a long walk for you to get home from the dumpster. . . ."

I think for a moment, and maybe Dad would come pick me up there? Or Grandpa or Grandma. Anyone, I guess. I think it would be nice to walk Mack home. The least I could do after she's tried so hard with Freddy the Frog and everything. And after she said I didn't care that she had to move.

"I'll get a ride from there," I say. "Ready to go?"

"Uh-huh." We pick up our backpacks and there's an eerie stillness to the air that's kind of nice, too. It's chilly and the leaves are beautiful and the track is empty and it feels like everything could be amazing here if people just wanted to see it that way. There is incredible stuff and beautiful stuff, but it gets so clouded over with the not-so-great stuff that people can't even see what's good anymore.

"Do you think Mr. Woodson is okay?" I ask. "It's weird he didn't show, right? And he didn't set up the big speakers, and the pom-poms didn't arrive. . . ."

"Nope. Not at all. Teachers do that all the time in Miller Creek. It's like they're only half working or they're preoccupied with other stuff. I don't really know."

"There has to be more to that story," I say, crunching leaves on the path and feeling satisfied every time.

We walk quietly the rest of the way and then Mack says, "All right, well, we're here. I'm not letting you come any farther."

We're standing in front of a condo development called Creekside but the C is missing so it looks like Reekside, which I'll admit is an unfortunate name for a condo development or pretty much anything.

"Mack, don't worry. I never judge people's homes. In Willets I had the smallest house of anyone. My best friend, Gracie, had a mansion, pretty much, with an in-ground pool and a Jacuzzi built into her deck, and my house had one and a half bathrooms, so seriously." I offer a reassuring smile. "Don't worry."

She folds her arms across her chest. "I don't care if you judge or don't judge or had three hundred and a half bathrooms, Natty. I still don't want you to see this dumpster trash. K? Thanks for walking me home. Now please leave."

"Honestly, the grassy areas look really nice," I say, peeking inside. "Lots of space to sunbathe and throw a

Frisbee or something."

"I've never thrown a Frisbee in my life."

She walks away from me, and I stand there for a minute or two before I realize I should call Dad or Grandma and Grandpa because we are kind of a far walk from their house.

"Hello?" Grandma answers the landline on the first ring.

"Hi, Grandma, it's Natty." I laugh. "Obviously. No one else calls you Grandma. Anyway, I decided to walk my friend Mack home to her new place; can you come pick me up? She lives in that condo development Creekside. Know where it is?"

"Huh? Say that again. Slow down, Natty. You talk so fast."

I sigh. "I need a ride home." I look at the intersection signs. "I'm at River Boulevard and Crane Avenue."

"Let me wake Grandpa. He needs to go to the pharmacy anyway."

"Clark!" she yells out. "Clark!"

She comes back to the phone. "Hold on, Natty. Let me go get him."

There's a thump when she puts the phone down on the counter; it's an old-fashioned, thick cordless one.

"Clark." I hear her muffled yell.

I sit down on the little strip of sidewalk because she

takes so long and my legs are tired. Finally, she gets back to the phone and tells me my grandfather is on his way, and he'll stop at the pharmacy on the way back.

"Your dad is out again with that teacher, so I think we'll go for pizza. Sound okay, Natty? I'm craving that pineapple pie you introduced me to."

My heart pounds like I just walked into something I didn't want to know about. "Sure, yeah, I love that one. Extra pineapple, K?"

"Okay. See you soon. Love you."

"Love you, too."

I ignore the part about Dad being out with the teacher and I ignore the tone in Grandma's voice where it seems like I should know what she's talking about. I ignore it all. My stomach tightens and I get scared that I'll need to get to a bathroom soon and won't have one close by, but I take deep breaths—in and out and in and out—and it seems to settle down. At least for now.

17

"HEY, MR. WOODSON," I SAY, popping my head into the doorway of his office the next day. I feel my phone vibrating in my pocket, but I ignore it for now. "Uh, just wanted to make sure everything's all right because you, um, missed the soccer game, and the speakers weren't up and—"

"Oh! Natty! I'm so sorry. And there's a delay with the pom-pom order . . . complications with the budget allotment." He shakes his head. "I don't have good excuses. Please forgive me. Did it go okay?"

"Oh yeah." I smile. "It went really well. People were definitely pumped up."

The phone rings and he holds up a finger that I should wait a minute, so I do, and I stand outside the office, but one minute turns into a really long time, and I need to get to practice.

I scribble a note on a piece of paper and run in quickly to leave it on his desk.

Mr. Woodson—Our next practice is happening in the gym right now. Come if you can! Thanks, Natty

I head to the gym, and surprisingly, everyone is already there when I walk in.

"So we all know the girls soccer game is Monday after school? Then we probably have one more event before the pep rally. We have a date set, but we need to start rallying the community!" I crack up. "Pun intended! Anyway, we'll get to that in a minute."

"Wait, so what are these events if they're not pep rallies?" Wade asks. "Please clarify."

He seems genuinely confused this time, not like he's making trouble.

"They're just, like, us getting everyone excited at games and meets and stuff," I explain. "We're going to try to be at most sporting events to cheer everyone on and pump everyone up!"

He nods. "I don't totally understand this."

"It's okay . . . but here's the thing. For the pep rally our job really is to just get the school and whole community excited, like, in general."

"Excited about what?" Braid asks.

"Our school! Miller Creek! Life! All the things." I bounce back and forth from foot to foot.

"But there's nothing to be excited about," Tape replies, finishing the wallet she's making out of duct tape.

"Gotta agree with her there," Marcus says, and then Lance shoves him with his arm.

"Dude," Lance says under his breath.

I ignore all that because there's no time for negativity now. Or ever. But definitely not now when I feel like we are honestly making progress. I keep looking at the door to see where Mack is. She wasn't in Advisory today and I couldn't find her at lunch and she didn't show for any other classes either.

Luna, Terra, and I lead the routine again for the group and demonstrate, step by step, and I think the repetition will really help. The more we do this, the better it will be!

We do the air trumpeting in, windmill over our heads, pointing up and across our bodies, the side steps and claps, the face display, shaking our fingers, the box step. Every time I see it, I love it more.

A few minutes into practice, Mack runs in wearing the whole Freddy the Frog suit. "Sorry I'm late! The pom-poms finally arrived!" she yells, and then drops a dilapidated-looking brown box onto the floor.

"Yay! Thank you, Mack! Amazing!"

After a few rounds of practice with the pom-poms,

I shout to the group, "This is all looking SO SO good! Remember to bring your posters, so we can hold them up in the bleachers during the game. The whole thing is going to be ahhhhh-maaaa-zinggggg!"

"Can she please stop saying that?" Tape sneers. "I still don't get why you're doing this, Natty. Like why you're trying so hard for a school you just started that obviously is not peppy at all."

"She's trying to convince her mom to move here, duh," Braid replies, and then her eyes bulge, almost like she just realized she said something she shouldn't have said.

My face immediately feels like it's on fire. I never told Braid that, or anyone that, I don't think.

But then I freeze. I remember.

I told Mack. Does this mean Mack told other people? Why would she do that?

I look over at her, but she obviously can't make real eye contact with me in the Freddy the Frog costume.

They all start whispering to each other.

"What? That is so weird. Why would her mom care about school spirit or whatever?" Kingsley asks.

I swallow hard to prevent the tears from creeping up. It feels like three globes are sitting on my throat. I ignore it. It's fine. They don't know what they're talking about. They don't understand the situation. I'm sure Mack told them when she was mad at me or something, but now things are fine and she brought the pom-poms. Things are fine. Totally fine.

I ignore it all and smile. "Anyway, you're all amazing. Sorry, I do use that word a lot! So, yeah, practice is over. Get psyched for the soccer game! So happy you're all part of this squad!"

"We're not a part of anything," Wade adds. "Remember we are doing this because we have to. Okay? But cool. Have a good day."

Mostly everyone walks out of the gym, even Mack. Terra and Luna are the only ones who stay.

"Um, Natty, we just wanted to hang back a second, and yeah, are you okay?" Terra asks, her eyebrows crinkled.

"Oh yeah, I'm totally fine. People say dumb stuff, but it honestly doesn't get to me." I shrug. "Seriously, today was great. Thank you sooo much again for coming up with that routine! It's really, really good and I love it."

"It was honestly so fun," Luna adds. "Maybe the three of us could, like, meet during lunch to practice and maybe even work on coming up with more routines? I mean, like, I know you guys are busy, and we don't need to, but, yeah, I just figured I'd mention it."

"What! That's an amazing idea! I'd love to." I look toward Terra. "Can you do that?"

"Um, yeah." She looks at the floor. "I mean, sometimes I want to just eat lunch with my friends and stuff, but yeah, I can totally come by." She takes her phone out of her pocket. "But I gotta run now. My mom is waiting. Byeee!"

Terra runs out of the gym and then Luna and I are just standing there.

"She's not as bad as everyone thinks she is, or as bad as Kingsley," Luna declares in a quiet tone. "We used to be best best best friends."

I nod. "Yeah. I hate when friendships change like that; it's so sad, but it's amazing you're, like, getting back together."

She laughs. "You make it sound like we're a couple! But yeah, I know what you mean."

Luna and I leave the gym together, and then she walks out to the late bus. I go to my locker before walking home, and also to check to see if there's a note from Mack, but there's nothing there.

I don't know why she left the gym with everyone, without talking to me. I don't know why she told them about my mom. I don't know anything, really. My stomach hurts so much I need to sit down against my locker. I can't let this one thing ruin the progress we made today. That would be really, really dumb.

On my way out of school, I pass by the main office and see Mr. Woodson in there with a few teachers. Through the glass, I can see him talking with his hands, emphatically. I can't hear what he's saying but he looks angry. Furious, even.

I move out of the way so they won't be able to see me,

and I hang back a moment in case he comes out. I want to thank him for the pom-poms.

He doesn't come out, though, and I start to head home before it really gets late. I need to call my mom and remind her about the pep rally again. If I keep mentioning it, it'll be harder and harder for her to say no.

"Hi, Mom," I say as soon as she answers.

"Oh, Natty! I was just thinking about you."

"Yay! Happy to hear that."

She sighs and then doesn't say anything.

"Mom? You okay?"

"Yeah." She sighs again. "My car is having issues and it's going to be tricky to get to Miller Creek and—"

"You can take the bus here. It's so easy. Also, it's not like you have to come tomorrow. You still have time before the pep rally to get it fixed."

"Natty, let's just see, okay? You know I love you, right?"

"Mmm-hmm." My throat gets tight, the way I imagine it would feel if it somehow got sunburned. My stomach gets that tight, twisted-up feeling again, worse than it was before.

She asks, "You know I'm proud of you, right?"

"Mmm-hmm." My whole body starts to feel even tighter, as if it's being wrung out like a wet towel. I swallow and swallow and swallow. I think I'm all cried out from before. I feel tears behind my eyes, but they don't pour out this time. I clear my throat and my words come out of my mouth like a squeak. "It's okay, Mom. I gotta go now, though, homework and stuff, lots going on here; it's all really great."

"Wonderful, Natty. Well, talk soon, and please know I love you."

"I know, Mom. I love you, too."

I end the call and put my phone in my pocket and stare straight ahead at the path in front of me. She's going to come one day. I know she will. But there's a tiny corner in the back of my brain with a voice saying, *But what if she doesn't? What if she never comes? What if I try and try and try and nothing ever changes?*

I kick a rock as hard as I can into the woods on the side of the street.

She'll come one day. I know it. I refuse to believe anything else.

I get to my house, and Mack is sitting there, on the front steps.

"Mack?" I say, startled. "What are you doing here?"

"Waiting for you."

"Right. Okay! Well, hi!"

"I need to confess something," she says, holding her head in her hands and staring at the ground. She looks like she's seen a ghost or something.

I sit down on the step next to her.

"I told everyone about your mom and that you're trying to get her to move here and that somehow the pep squad has something to do with it. They were all talking about it one day on the bus line, like why anyone would start something like that, and I never have anything to say, and so I just said it, and I'm so sorry." She pauses, sniffling. "I've been so sick about it. I thought being the dumb mascot and then stalking the UPS driver and bringing in the pom-poms would make up for it, but I still feel so bad." She doesn't make eye contact with me.

My stomach feels twisted up again, but I take a deep breath and then exhale. "Mack, it's fine. It's the truth. I mean, everyone didn't *need* to know, but it's okay that they do. Seriously."

She looks up at me finally. "Really?"

"Yes, Mack. It's okay. It's all good."

"It is? How is even *this* all good?"

"Because it's the truth, and maybe it'll help the squad feel closer to me. I don't know, whatever, but it's all good!" I smile, forcing the words to come out energetic, forcing myself to stay upbeat.

"You're the weirdest person I have LITERALLY ever met." Mack laughs. "But, cool, glad we're okay and stuff."

"Cool." I smile. "How's the condo?"

"You mean the overflowing-dumpster-on-fire condo from hell?"

"I don't know because I haven't seen it yet. It's all relative, Mack. Someone could think my grandparents' house is an overflowing-dumpster-on-fire house from hell. I'm sure most of the people in Willets, where I used to live, would. It's really fancy there. My friend Gracie can't even believe I sleep on a futon in an attic, but you know what?" I look right into her eyes.

"What?"

"It's cozy, and I like it, and the attic is really private; it's kind of like I have my own apartment up there. I think it's cool."

"But that's because you think everything is cool and great and 'all good.'"

I shrug. "Doesn't cost more to be positive, Mack. Doesn't cost more to be positive."

She huffs and rolls her eyes. "I'm leaving. You're still as annoying as you were yesterday. But I'm glad you're not mad at me and I'm glad you don't hate me."

"K, see you tomorrow!" I say, cheerful.

She starts heading down the front path to the side-walk.

"Wait, Mack! You can't walk all the way home alone from here!" I yell.

"Don't call it home!" she yells back. "And yes, I can. I walked here on my own and it was fine. There's a back way I didn't remember. We're actually closer than you think!"

"We are?" I feel sort of warm and cozy after she says that. "What great news!"

"Calm down, Natty. Bye."

"Bye!" I yell again.

I walk inside and Grandma's making spaghetti and meatballs and they smell so good. Grandpa's asleep in the recliner and I peek around for my dad, but I don't see him.

I head up to the attic and lie down, and keep reminding myself there's not a time limit for my mom to come. It's not like I had to convince her by the end of September. Or even November. Or even by the first pep rally. We'll have other pep rallies after this one, and many other events!

It'll take however long it takes and that's okay. We can't rush these things. As much as I want to and want her to be here as soon as humanly possible, I know I can't rush it.

18

"DINNER!" I HEAR GRANDMA CALLING from downstairs. She wakes me up from the deepest kind of sleep. It almost feels like morning right now. I don't even remember passing out. I don't even know how long I slept for.

I run downstairs and find Grandpa already at the table. He really wakes up fast when food is in his future.

"Where's Dad?" I ask.

"I'm not sure," Grandma says, facing the stove. "He's been out and about lately. I think he's really trying to find his people here. Oh! And he's ending medical leave from work early, and he got permission to work remotely, too! All good news!"

"That's great," I say.

"He seems to be doing better, doesn't he?" Grandma asks, turning around.

"For sure!"

We all sit down and dig into Grandma's spaghetti and meatballs. She made garlic bread, too, and a salad with tomatoes and mozzarella and croutons. It's a full-on feast.

Dad will be sad he's missing it.

"So are you guys getting excited? Our first official pep rally is coming up!" I clap and then do a little dance in my kitchen chair. "I emailed the mayor to ask him to speak! You're gonna come, right?"

"Are we supposed to attend that kind of thing?" Grandma asks, and then takes a long sip of lemonade. "Isn't that for the students?"

I nod. "Yeah, it is, but community members can come, too. We're encouraging people to come, and it's not only a pep rally for the junior high. It's a pep rally for the town, too. It's like Miller Creek pride. I'm really trying to build on that. Actually, maybe you can help me hang some flyers when you're out around town!"

"Isn't it great what she's doing, Clark?" Grandma asks. "Truly a making-lemonade-out-of-lemons thing . . . and not just because you're drinking my homemade raspberry lemonade right now!"

Grandma laughs, and then Grandpa and I do, too, because her laugh is seriously the most contagious laugh I've ever heard.

"It's not really a lemons thing, Grandma. That makes this situation seem bad and it's not. Sure, unconventional, unexpected. But bad? Not at all."

Grandma and Grandpa look at each other in a weird kind of way, the way they always look at one another when they can't quite figure me out. It happens sort of often lately. I think they're just not used to having a kid in the house.

We're all halfway through our second helpings of spaghetti and meatballs when Dad walks into the house through the kitchen door.

"Hi. Sorry I'm late." He smiles and sits down and spreads his napkin over his lap. "How was everyone's day?"

Grandpa goes on for a while about this show he saw on TV about life on other planets and how we really need to be focusing on discovering what's out there. Grandma tells us about her bridge game and how Nancy is considering assisted living. And I tell everyone more about our new routine and the plans for the first-ever school pep rally.

"It's really happening?" Dad asks.

"Yeah! Of course! It's on the community calendar and everything." I take another piece of garlic bread. "You can Google it and see!"

"Oh, I thought I heard there may be a conflict . . . and I was worried it would be canceled . . . and . . ." His voice trails off and he scoops some more spaghetti onto his plate.

"From who?" I ask, interrupting him.

Then Grandpa and Grandma do that look-at-each-other thing again and Dad gets in on it, too. They're all acting a little weird right now.

"Um, I don't even remember," Dad stammers. "Anyway, glad it's happening. I'll definitely be there."

I wonder if they're being weird because of the Mom thing, and the mystery about her coming.

"I'm not sure exactly when Mom's gonna come," I blurt out. "It's still up in the air."

"Okay." Dad smiles his trying-to-be-sympathetic smile. He doesn't seem surprised by this news. "Good to know."

"It's always good to know stuff, I think. Better than not knowing." I take another half plate of salad even though I'm starting to get really full.

"Very deep, Natty. You could be a motivational speaker," Grandpa says.

"I've considered it. Honestly. I think I could be, too."

"Oh, Natty, you're one of a kind," my dad says. He wipes the corners of his mouth with the napkin and then clears his plate. "I'm going to head out, I think. So if I'm not back by the time you're in bed, sweet dreams, Nat."

"Thanks." My heart sinks a little when he says he's heading out again but I really don't know why. I should be glad he's happy and not sleeping all the time.

Grandma, Grandpa, and I stay at the table for a few more minutes after he leaves, and I wait for them to say a little bit about where he's going, but they don't. I help load the dishwasher and then go up to my attic room to finish homework.

I'm halfway through my English essay on *Of Mice and Men* when I get a text from Mack.

Mack: made it to Dumpster Condo from Hell safely.

Just in case you were worried

Me: Oh good to hear!

Mack: I'll show you the back way tomorrow

I lay in bed that night thinking about Mack and what she told everyone, but then how great it was with Terra and Luna and the routine. Such an up-and-down day. Not knowing when Mom will visit but Dad seeming happy.

Everything feels all over the place, but generally it seems like it's all moving in the right direction.

I'm not giving up on Mom moving here. No way. Not at all.

From: Natty Blaken
To: Miller Creek Pep Squad
Subject: STUFF

Hello, Peppy People! Happy Sunday! A few reminders.

We have the girls soccer game tomorrow! Come practice the routine, wear green and gray, and bring your posters!

Pep Rally is coming up soon! I printed out flyers to hang around town, so please take a few and hang them wherever you see a good spot! It's on the Miller Creek online community calendar! Hoping to have a huge crowd!

Our regular meetings/rehearsals are every Tuesday after school!

Terra, Luna, and I will be meeting to practice and also choreograph new routines during lunch as often as we can! Come join us for that, too, if you want!

Forever peppy,

Natty

"Homeschooling could be cool, though," Wade says to Luna on Monday morning, loud enough for most of the whole hallway to hear. They're sitting on the floor, their backs against the vending machines by the gym. They're sharing a bag of Twizzlers and a bag of pretzels.

"Not for me," Luna replies. "My family cannot handle that. Our internet is broken three hundred and sixty-two days per year, no joke."

"I'm just saying it would be cool to do our own thing during the day," he adds.

After that, I can't hear what they're saying, but I'm really curious. I can't figure out why they'd be talking about homeschooling. If they were to go that route, would they still be able to be in the pep squad? I'm not sure.

I head to my locker and then Mack gets to school a minute later looking the most disheveled I've ever seen her. She definitely didn't brush her hair, and her green sweatshirt has a mysterious splotchy stain by the collar.

She sprawls out on the floor in front of the lockers, resting her head on her backpack like a pillow. "Need to nap before Advisory. Shhh."

"So after the pep rally, our commitment is complete?" Wade asks, standing in front of me, appearing out of the blue.

"Um, well, I hope not." I try as hard as I can not to laugh at his unique adultish way of speaking. "We're gonna be at most of the sporting events after the pep rally. . . . I mean, as many as we can, and there are spring sports, too, so yeah." I stand up straighter against my locker.

"Wait, so is it a whole-year thing or not?" Tape asks. "Lunch Girl, it's getting a little more fun, okay, I'll admit that. But this isn't like our life goal."

She admitted it's getting a little more fun! That's huge!

I giggle for a second. "That's okay. Well, let's just get to the pep rally and make it awesome. Then we can talk."

"Natty, I'll also admit that you're growing on me a little, but also, like, you're not in charge of us," Braid chimes in. "You know that, right?"

"Yeah, you're in charge of you. You're in charge of your destiny. . . ." I widen my eyes, and even though I firmly believe what I'm saying, I laugh so they get the sense I'm not taking myself too seriously.

Braid, Tape, and Wade walk away, but Luna stays and

a minute later, Terra shows up at my locker.

"Wanna do a little early-morning practice?" she asks us.

"Yes!" I jump up, and then reach my hand down toward Luna to pull her up.

We start doing the routine in the hallway, making all the side steps really small so we don't knock into anyone.

I'm halfway through it when I notice Mack sitting up, her back against the locker, staring at us.

"Isn't this routine looking SO good?" I ask her.

"Um, you're dancing in the middle of the hallway right now." She gets up, throws her backpack over her shoulder and walks away. Terra and Luna sort of eye-roll at each other and a second later the bell rings. We all walk in different directions, and when I get to Advisory, Ms. Lamlot's in the doorway greeting everyone.

"Natty! I just wanted to say that you do everything with such enthusiasm, it's a joy to watch." She smiles.

"Ms. Lamlot! Thank you!" I smile back. "Pep Squad has another event today—girls soccer. Come!"

"Oh, I will try! For sure, I will try."

I walk into class and Mack is staring at me like she wants to rip my head off. "I just have to say that it's so cringy that you're best friends with Lilian and Terra now. Way to ditch me after I was your first friend here. . . ."

"What?" I laugh. "What do you mean?"

"Meeting to practice during lunch, hanging out on the weekends, dancing in the hallway together . . . You don't need me. You're friends with the cool kids now. Well, Terra is cool. Lilian, not so much."

"Mack." I pause and try to move my chair a little closer to hers. "Sure, I'm friends with them, but I'm friends with you, too. Come to one of the extra practices, okay? At least before the pep rally. We'll all hang. It'll be fun."

"Whatever, Natty, just stop talking." Mack puts her head on the desk again. "It's hard to be friends with you when you never acknowledge what I'm saying or what I'm going through, you know that, right?"

I'm about to reply when Ms. Lamlot starts making some announcements, but I can't focus on anything she's saying. She has a bouquet of daisies on her desk and I swear it's the same bouquet I saw my dad holding when he came in late for spaghetti and meatballs.

My head pounds. *What is happening? What is happening? What is happening?*

Nope. No time for that.

Eyes on the prize.

One step in front of the other.

Good vibes only.

My stomach twists into a pretzel and I slump forward in my seat. I sneakily take a saltine out of my bag and chew it so quietly Ms. Lamlot doesn't notice.

Everything is fine.

From: Natty Blaken
To: Miller Creek Junior High Coaches
Subject: PEP RALLY

Hiiiii! If we haven't met yet, I want to introduce myself. I'm Natty Blaken and I'm in charge of the Miller Creek Junior High Pep Squad. Our first pep rally is coming up in two weeks, and I want to make sure all the sports teams are there! All the athletes should come in uniforms, we'll introduce them, and then be ready to dance around a little to my PEP RALLY PLAYLIST! Feel free to email back with any questions.

Thank you!
Forever Peppy,
Natty J. Blaken

After school, I head out to the soccer field, carrying the three different signs I made. They're all in green and gray and say, "MILLER CREEK SOCCER RULES! GO, MILLER CREEK FROGS! WE ARE THE FROGS!"

Terra and Luna are already there practicing, and I think back to what Mack was saying earlier. I guess the two of them are pretty close, which is pretty shocking after how much they seemed to hate each other just a few weeks ago. But it's great that they're close! And, yeah, I feel like I'm actually friends with them, but I'm friends with Mack, too.

"Hey," I say to Luna and Terra as soon I make it over to them. "Where's everyone else?"

I look around for Wade, Braid, and Tape, Kingsley, Rowan, and Lance and his friends.

"Oh, Natty, bad news," Terra replies, sounding defeated. "Kingsie and Ro are coming late. They're probably gonna miss our routine. So lame, but they didn't finish the math test third period and they said this is the only time they can finish it." She makes a sad face.

I look over at Luna. "Oh yeah, the rest of my crew isn't coming today either. They realized Woodson never really checks since he's MIA all the time, and they're tired, so they're bailing on the game." She pauses. "I'm sorry, Natty, but no need for downer energy, right? Attitude is everything and we will BRING IT TODAY."

I force a smile, but it feels like there are a million tiny

toothpicks going into my skin right now. We worked so hard to prepare for today, and most of the squad isn't even here! It's like the day our routine isn't ready, we have the people to do it, and the day our routine is actually awesome, the people don't show up!

I wonder if Lance and his friends will come.

"Yeah, totally, for sure." I start talking, and my voice catches in my throat. "I mean, I wish they were here, but yeah, you're right. We'll crush it anyway!"

I peek around the side of the bleachers, looking for Mack, kind of thinking she's gonna bail, too.

"We'll just cheer so loud, and it'll be fabulous. I mean, the routine is our creation, so we'll obviously be amazing," I tell them, my words catching in my throat again. I'm trying so hard to hold back tears. "Small but mighty, ya know? We can totally handle this on our own! We'll do our back-and-forth cheer after the routine, and at least we have the pom-poms now!"

They nod and then glance at each other.

"Sure you're okay, Natty?" Terra asks.

"Yeah!" I say, way too loud. "Of course! I'm great! And I am the LUCKIEST to have you two on this squad." I clap. "Oh, wait, be back in a minute. I need to grab the pom-poms from the gym office."

As I'm walking away, I hear Luna whisper to Terra, "She is definitely not okay, but she always keeps everything so positive. It's weird, right?"

I'm too far away to hear Terra's reply. I *am* okay, though, that's the thing! I mean, yeah, am I disappointed the others are bailing? Of course. But that doesn't mean we won't have a great event with a small group!

I feel my phone vibrating in my pocket, and without even looking to see who it is, I say hello.

"OMG, Natty! You answered," Gracie says. "I need to talk to you. Everything is crazy! The Core moms are saying it was my mom's fault that your mom left and you moved away. They're blaming everything on her all of a sudden, like 'cuz we were the closest and stuff. I don't even know."

"Wait, say that again," I tell her. "It's so hard to hear, we're about to have a pep squad event for a soccer game."

"It's a whole thing, Natty." She pauses. "You can't talk now?"

"I'm so sorry. I really can't."

"Ugh, Natty. You're always busy. Call me later. Bye." She runs her words together and hangs up before I have a chance to say anything else.

I honestly have no idea what Gracie was saying, and I have no clue how The Core moms could be that mean.

I get back to the soccer field with the pom-poms, quickly check to see if Gracie texted me anything, and when I see the clock on my phone, I realize it's time to start!

Mr. Woodson is nowhere to be found, but at least the speakers have been set up this time. I'll have to thank him for that and thank the tech staff, too!

"I was all stressed before because I couldn't figure out how we could carry our pom-poms and our posters at the same time," I say to Terra and Luna before we go out to the field. "But then I realized—pom-poms under our armpits! Signs in our hands, then we drop the signs on the side of the bleachers and hold out the pom-poms."

They look at me confused, like they're not sure this makes sense at all.

"Natty, what?" Terra shakes her head. "We can't do that because the music starts before we get out there. Remember? We air trumpet out to the music?" she says, sort of seeming confused that I didn't realize this. But I'm all twisted up that most of the squad isn't here. I'm trying not to let the bad vibes take over. Trying as hard as I can.

She continues. "We should just leave the posters by the bleachers now and use them when we're cheering from the crowd. That way we can hold our pom-poms out like actual trumpets while we march out with the music." Terra pauses. "It'll look really cool!"

"Agreed!" Luna shouts, and starts laughing. "No armpit pom-poms today! Or ever!"

I crack up. "Okay, you're both right. Glad I have you two to help me figure this stuff out!"

I turn on the music on my phone, and it actually connects with the speaker! We air trumpet with our pom-poms out onto the field and we start the routine.

Our marching is in perfect unison. Literally. Like we are basically the Rockettes right now, and the windmill and side steps are perfect, too.

My heart is pounding—half nervous, half exhilarated.

We're at the by-our-sides-emoji-hands part when Lance and his friends run to catch up with us and join in as if they've known this routine their whole lives. They're actually, like, really getting into it! They're sort of laughing the whole time, almost falling over, like they can't take it seriously, but then their box steps and claps are perfectly together.

I lose focus, watching Lance and his friends and then I fall out of sync with everyone.

Get it together, Natty. Follow along. Everyone is watching you.

I'm finally catching up, and almost in rhythm again, when out of the corner of my eye, I see Freddy the Frog running onto the field, exactly when she's supposed to come out. There's something about Freddy bouncing into the routine that gets the whole crowd up and clapping and dancing along with this.

At the end of the song, Terra, Luna, and I start the

cheer: "We are Miller Creek! Miller Miller. Creek Creek Creek," I say.

Luna and Terra and Lance and his friends all jump right in with the exact right reply at the exact right time: "Go, Frogs! Dance around! Go, Frogs!"

And that's when the whole crowd erupts from their seats, clapping and cheering like this is the best thing they've ever seen!

"Natty!" Terra screeches, pulling me in for a sideways hug as we walk over to the bleachers. "That was awesome. The best it's ever been! Wasn't it? I mean, the whole thing, like epic-level awesome!" She wipes some sweat off her forehead with the back of her hand.

"It was!" I smile so hard it almost hurts. "It really was!"

Luna runs up and links arms with me on one side, and Terra links arms with me on the other, and we walk like that the rest of the way to the bleachers. We hold up our posters and keep cheering from the front row.

"Mack!" I say, leaning forward a little so I can talk to her down the row. "Did you see how everyone got so excited when you came out?"

"You mean when Freddy came out?"

I laugh. "Well, yeah."

"I saw it." She pauses. "It was cool. Don't go crazy."

A Miller Creek player scores a goal and we all stand up and cheer as loud as we can. Then I see Kingsley and

Rowan coming over to the bleachers. Too little, too late. I don't want them to pour any sour straws into these perfect strawberry shoelaces of a day.

"OMG! So sorry we missed the whole routine?" Kingsley sing-songs when she gets to us, and makes an over-the-top frowny face.

"Ugh, I'm really sorry." Rowan does the same thing, but she actually seems mostly genuine.

"You missed it and it was really good," Terra says, not making eye contact with them. "Just sit. You could have finished the math test tomorrow. You have a commitment to this squad."

"Well, I guess *she's a Valentina*," Rowan says, and then Kingsley falls into laughter. No clue what that means, must be some private joke between them.

But it doesn't matter because Terra ignores it and looks down the row at Lance and his friends. "And you four. Yeah, you know the routine, and you're like spookily good at it, but if you show up late and then half fall over from laughing, no one will take us seriously." She pauses. "Get it together or leave the squad!"

She stares at them and stops talking and no one responds.

I think we're all pretty stunned after that.

It feels like this event just unlocked something major, a whole part of Terra I didn't know was there, and she may not have known was there either.

Every time someone scores a goal, we all stand up and cheer and shake our pom-poms and Freddy dances around in front of the bleachers.

And I know half the squad bailed and two key people missed the whole routine.

But something absolutely, positively amazing is happening here.

21

THE NEXT DAY, I'M AT my locker putting my books away before lunch, and I quickly check my phone. I have five texts from Gracie. I can't believe I forgot to call her back after the soccer game.

Gracie: Natty what is happening?

Gracie: you never call me back and I really need to talk to you

Gracie: are you ok?

Gracie: I'm worried & also mad

Gracie: kk love you

"Hey, Natty," Luna says, coming up behind me and draping an arm over my shoulders. "Can we talk for a sec?"

"Of course!" I smile, putting my phone back in my locker and trying to ignore the Gracie texts for a moment.

Someone texting should never take priority over someone who's here, right next to me, in person. Plus Gracie's vibes are so negative lately; I can't deal with them and I definitely cannot let them bring me down, especially when things are going so great with the pep squad, and life in general here. "What's up?"

"So, like, I think we need to try harder with Braid, Tape, and Wade." She looks me right in the eyes. "They only had to do this because of the whole basketball-court thing but now Mr. Woodson is MIA anyway, so they're not gonna finish. They'll keep bailing on events, they'll need another punishment, plus the squad needs them as members." She pauses. "Also, like, I kind of think the pep squad is awesome, and I want them to realize that, too."

I nod, trying to take in everything she's saying. "I know what you mean and I am so happy you think it's awesome and I really want them to get into it, too. Can we discuss the best way to make that happen?" I ask. "I feel kinda clueless about how to, like, connect with them."

"Yeah, I can help." She smiles. "I'm starving, though, and I can't think clearly right now. It's pizza today, which is, like, the only acceptable school lunch here."

We start walking to the cafeteria and I realize there's something else I want to talk to her about. "So, like, what happened with you and Terra, back in the day? And I guess Mack, too? Seems like there's so much drama between everyone," I say.

She shakes her head. "Oh, it's so dumb. Like, all stupid kid stuff. In kindergarten until like second grade, Terra, Mack, and I were best friends, and it's true that I did puke in Terra's sprinkler at her end-of-the-year party in third grade, so for a while people called me 'Lilian Upchuck.' That's when I was going by Lilian. . . ." Her voice trails off and then she continues. "I called Terra 'Terra the Terrible' for a while after that, but it didn't catch on because she's just so likable . . . and Mack is just Mack. Like, as kids, her weirdness was fine, pulling out her eyelashes, wearing the same shirt every day, but as we got older, she just seemed, like, eerie, giving off a spooky vibe." She shrugs. "So then, like, she distanced herself and became a huge loner, and Terra became best friends with Kingsley and Rowan, and in fifth grade, they just sort of became the popular group with a few other random girls but mostly with this girl Valentina, but then they sort of tortured her and she ended up switching schools, and that was that."

I nod, trying to listen and understand. Now that comment about being a Valentina makes a little more sense. "And then what about you?"

"Well, we all just drifted and I couldn't totally find my people after that, and Tape and Braid were nice to me. They were originally just Theresa and Bailey, by the way, and then Wade found his way to us because he never really connected with the boys, and we just became a crew." She pauses. "I don't even know if they're really my people. I'm not so into how they want to vandalize stuff and sort of get in trouble for fun. Know what I mean?"

"Yeah, definitely." I want her to keep talking and telling me all this stuff because it's fascinating and really helps me understand all of them. But we eventually get to the cafeteria for lunch and sit down at our table.

"Lunch Girl!" Wade says as soon as we get there. His hair is actually down today, not pulled back in his little ponytail. "Lunch Girl is actually at lunch! We were gonna have to change your name since you've barely been here lately. . . ."

I giggle. "Yeah, sorry, I've been trying to work on stuff at lunch lately: the routine, brainstorming ideas for the pep rally, emailing the coaches, making flyers on the library computer . . . things like that."

Braid tears open a bag of chips. "Want one? I accidentally—not so accidentally—knocked into the vending machine when I was pissed at my mom this morning and a bag fell out, totally free!"

"Sure. Barbecue chips are one of my favorite varieties," I reply. "I like all chips, though. Except salt and vinegar. Too salty. Too vinegary, too."

"Natty, you have commentary on everything! I love it!" Luna nudges me with her elbow. "You need a podcast or something!"

"Ooh, good idea! You guys could be my first guests."

"Not a chance," Tape replies, sticking her plastic spork into the cafeteria pizza. "This is the grossest lunch. It looks like jail food, right?"

"What? Tape! Pizza is the only good meal here," Luna argues. "Also, I don't think they serve pizza in jail. Just a hunch."

"I agree with Tape." Wade holds up a slice and none of the cheese jiggles off. It's just sort of stuck there, on the bread. "And yet Lunch Girl brings her fancy wraps and sandwiches and homemade cookies to school, and she picks us to sit with so we have to see her munching on them, all fancy. . . ." He shakes his head. "It's an injustice!"

"Leave Lunch Girl alone," Luna adds, draping an arm over my shoulders. "Also, can we just call her Natty now? We know her name."

"Want half of my wrap?" I ask Wade. "It's not that fancy. Just turkey, American cheese, some mayo, some lettuce."

"That lettuce is fancy," Tape says. "It's romaine, not iceberg, right?"

I nod.

"See. Fancy," she says, all smug. "I know my lettuces."

I never realized bringing lunch would be such a big deal. I would be fine with the cafeteria lunch, but Grandma actually really likes cooking and preparing stuff so she just does it, without me even asking. I never thought of these lunches as fancy. Not at all.

"My grandma's just bored," I explain. "So she makes me lunch."

They ignore me after that and go back to discussing this skate park that's opening soon, and even though none of them skate, they think it'll be really fun to hang out there.

"Speaking of grandmas," Luna says a few moments later, when I really thought we were off the topic of lunch. "Mine is coming to the pep rally. She's so pumped I'm actually doing a school activity! Natty, she saw one of your flyers outside the pharmacy!"

"Your grandma is coming?" I shriek, and they all stare at me and motion that I should quiet down immediately.

"Yup! A little weird but whatever, she doesn't have many activities," Luna explains.

"Not weird at all! My grandparents are coming, too. And I'm so happy she saw my flyer!"

"Whoa, this is becoming some kind of Miller Creek elderly reunion," Wade adds, cracking himself up.

"It's gonna be great, and also my grandparents aren't that old," I explain. "I'm sure Luna's grandma is young, too."

Luna bites into her slice of pizza and then talks while still chewing. "I have no clue how old she is."

"Well, either way, I am psyched! This is going to be soooo great! The community is really getting involved and excited about this!" I open my tinfoil packet of home-made cookies and see that Grandma gave me five today. One for everyone. "Here! Happy to share my cookies!" I spread out the foil and show them all. "Take one."

"Lunch Girl, you can be annoying sometimes, but I gotta say—you've really mastered lunch," Wade says.

"Thanks, Wade." I smile.

And that's when it hits me. A way to really try to connect with them, what Luna brought up earlier! "I can bring you all lunch stuff, you know. Like I said, my grandma likes to cook and she loves taking care of people. . . ."

"Really?" Tape asks, adjusting the strip of duct tape on her forehead, her eyes as wide as I've ever seen them.

"I think we should take her up on this," Braid adds. "If she's gonna be at our table and we have to suffer through her stupid pep squad, we might as well get some good food out of it."

"I kind of agree." Luna shrugs but then laughs like she's kidding, and she's happy I'm at their table. "JK. Natty's my girl now. And the pep squad is *def* not stupid; it's really fun. If you guys actually showed up and, like, gave it a chance, you'd see how awesome it is."

"Yes! To all of that!" I do a little air-cheer with my hands. "And also, my grandma is going to be SO excited!" I do a quick little clap. "Lunch. IT IS ON."

22

AFTER SCHOOL, I WAIT OUTSIDE the office to talk to Mr. Woodson and he's in a meeting again. I don't care, though; I'll wait as long as it takes. I need to update him that we added the girls volleyball game to our list of events and that we'll need the speakers set up in the gym. Plus I need to update him on some details about the pep rally and hand him some of the flyers I made to put up around town.

His meeting goes on forever, it seems—the janitor is mopping the halls and wiping down the lockers and I'm still sitting there on the little wooden bench outside the office. It's okay, though—I managed to get all of my homework done, even study for my Spanish test and complete the math packet we were given for extra credit.

It's kind of amazing what you can accomplish when you're forced to sit in one spot for a while.

It's almost five when Mr. Woodson and the other teachers finally leave the office.

"Natty!" he says, shocked to see me. "What are you still doing here?"

"Mr. Woodson! Hi! I just wanted to update you! I know you're busy and haven't been able to make the pep squad meetings and the events, but we're soooo excited. Things are going great! I added an event for us last-minute—girls volleyball tomorrow." I pause to catch my breath. "Just want to make sure the speakers are set up in the gym for that! Also, all the kids have been coming, so please make sure they get the credit! And yeah, the pep rally is coming up soon, too!"

"Oh, right. The pep rally." He looks at the group of teachers who have suddenly stopped walking, and they all sort of stare at each other for what feels like a very ominous few seconds.

"I know the school day is set to end early for it," I say, "and everyone will come out to the football field after the last bell, and I already checked with the main office staff that they'll make a few extra announcements throughout the day, and the squad is ready and prepared to do our thing. . . . All of the sports teams will be coming out in their uniforms. It's on the Miller Creek online community calendar, and I reached out to the mayor of Miller Creek so he can announce us. . . ."

He looks off into the distance like he's searching for answers far at the end of the hallway. "Natty, I think you've really thought of everything. This club and this school and, frankly, this town are exceedingly lucky you relocated here."

"Aw, Mr. Woodson. Thanks!" I shrug, feeling extra light and carefree all of a sudden. "I'm so happy to hear you say that."

"You should head home, though. It's getting late." He puts his hands in his pockets.

"Right, yeah." I smile. "Okay. Well, then, see you tomorrow!"

"Good night, Natty. Be safe."

When I get home, Mack's waiting for me on the front steps again. I have no idea how long she's been out here since it's after six and I'm just getting here. I wonder if she needs to use the bathroom or anything.

"I overheard your little delinquent friends talking on the bus line, and your grandma's making lunches for all of them now?" she asks, her eyes squinty tight, like she's forcing herself not to cry. Sometimes I think Mack may be a spy. "And I'm your actual friend and you never offered for her to make me lunches. I've told you I don't eat ALL DAY LONG. Also, you don't even ask how I'm doing in the new place. First you hang out with Luna and Terra and don't include me, you dance around with them like you're BFFs, and do you even realize you totally ignore everything I'm going through?" She sniffles. I think she may be on the verge of tears.

I sit down next to her. "Oh, Mack. It's okay. I just said that because they're constantly talking about my home-made lunches and my grandma is actually really bored. And I also thought bringing them lunch might give them the energy boost they need to really do great with the squad. She'll make you lunch, too. No problem. She's very, very bored and loves to do stuff for people." I laugh.

"This isn't funny, Natty. You think it's all a big joke how you have people looking out for you and homemade lunch every day." She stares right into my eyes. "You're privileged and you don't even see it. It's not okay. You can't go through life not realizing your privilege."

I pause a second before I answer. I almost remind her I sleep on a futon in an old attic but actually it's very comfortable and I don't mind it, and I prefer my attic room, so there would be no reason for me to say that.

"I do realize it," I say softly.

"I'm sorry to say this, but you're not a good friend. You don't even show that you care at all." She pauses. "I don't think you know *how* to care."

I shuffle my feet on the pavement and start to feel antsy. I need to get inside and call Gracie back, make some more posters for the volleyball game and the pep rally, and tell Grandma about the lunches. "I do care." I move a little closer to her on the step, and she turns away from me. "Tell me what you want for lunch. My grandma can make anything. Her brie and apple sandwiches are restaurant quality, for real."

"I've obviously never had brie. I've barely even heard of brie."

"Well, it's sort of an acquired taste," I add.

I stretch my legs out in front of me and shake out my left foot since it's just fallen asleep. "You're pretty much the star of the whole squad. You know that, right? A mascot is a big deal. A huge deal. We've never had one before. I don't even think the high school has one. This is going to change the way everyone feels about the school and the town." I pause. "I am sooooo excited."

"You need to calm down. I've told you this a million times. You're just gonna get disappointed if your expectations are always so high."

"Not true."

She rolls her eyes. "Anyway, back to lunch." She pauses and smiles, and it seems like she's feeling a little more relaxed now. "I'd like a turkey and Swiss on a roll with lettuce and a little mustard, and a bag of those kettle chips you always have would be great, too." She wiggles her fingers in the air. "I'll bring my water bottle. No need for a drink. Thanks."

"Yup. On it." I smile. "Get home safe. I'm glad you'll be really well nourished for all the events going forward. I hadn't thought about it before this, but obviously you need to be well fed."

"Obviously."

Mack gets up and walks away and I head inside. Grandma's going to be busy tonight, but I know she's up for the challenge. It'll be great.

"Grandma!" I yell, hearing the screen door close behind me. "Grandma!"

"Natty! Hi!" She comes out from the downstairs bathroom with a bucket of cleaning supplies, some strands of her hair stuck to her forehead. "What's going on?" she asks.

"Well, first of all put down the bucket and everything; take your time. . . ." I smile. I don't want to rush her or frazzle her, especially when I'm asking for something so big.

"Everything okay, Natty?" she asks, suspicious sounding. "I'm just finishing scrubbing the tub."

"Oh yeah, everything is great. I'm going to relax. Meet me in the den."

I sit down on the couch while Grandpa snoozes in the recliner. I stare out the window at the changing leaves. I never sit in here, probably because someone is always asleep, but it's a lovely room.

"So, what can I do for you, Natty?" Grandma asks a few minutes later, sitting down next to me on the couch.

"Wellll . . . you know how you love to make lunch for me?"

She slow-nods.

"Welll . . . everyone at my lunch table has been eyeing my lunches. It turns out most kids, and I mean all the kids, get the school lunch. And they're all kind of jealous . . . so I kind of offered that you'd make lunch for my table, I guess, for, like, as long as you can and for Mack, too. You know, the girl who is always sitting on our front steps." I lift my shoulders. "Please say yes, please say yes. I just want to do something nice for all of them. I try to spread positive vibes, but I think a lot of it just comes down to a nourishing, delicious lunch. That's what they need."

She exhales. "I do love to prepare lunches. . . . It took forever to pass the free lunch program here and people say the food's not so great."

"Yeah." I sigh. "The lunches are reeeeally gross."

Grandma stares at me and slowly shakes her head. "How many lunches are we talking about here?"

"Oh." I perk up, thinking she's going to say yes. "Like five, I guess. Six including me."

She takes a deep breath and exhales again. "Okay, let me run to the store. Make a list of all the kinds of sandwiches the kids might want so I can get the ingredients. Okay?"

"Yes, yes, of course! Thank you sooo much." I reach over and pull her into a super tight hug. "This means sooo much to me, Grandma. Thank you!"

I'm so fired up about Grandma making the lunches, but then I remember I have to call Gracie back and I feel like she might be mad it's taken me this long. I run up to the attic and click her name in the list of favorites in my phone, and when she appears on the screen, I say, "Hi, I'm so sorry it's taken me so long to call you."

I smile to hopefully soften things a little.

"Natty, what is going on with you? You're being such a bad friend."

My heart sinks a little and I hesitate to reply. "Oh my god, no. Don't say that." It feels extra bad because Mack sort of said the same thing before.

"I will say that because I don't get what's going on with you." She rubs her eyes and curls herself into a ball on her paisley cushioned window seat. "You take forever to write back to my texts; you never FaceTime. I don't get it. I'm telling you how hard things are, and you're, like, ignoring everything!"

I look away from the screen, but I can't make eye contact with her right now. "I'm sorry. I'm just really preoccupied with getting settled here, and there's so much

I want to do. . . . And yeah, I'm sorry. I guess I don't have a good reason."

"I've told you so many times that things are really hard here! And I was there for you when things were hard for you last year," she says, almost yelling now. "Don't you get it? Our friends are pushing me away, and pushing my mom away, too. It's like they decided they just don't want to be friends with people all of a sudden."

"But I don't get that," I say, pulling my blanket up to my neck, suddenly freezing. "Everyone loves you. You're amazing. Your mom, too."

"I don't know what's happening, Natty. Or why it's happening. It just feels really bad."

"I think if you just, like, pretend everything is normal, and, like, really make an effort to have a good attitude and stuff, it'll be okay, Gracie. . . . I really do. Sometimes it's just about walking with your head held high and thinking positive thoughts. Sometimes it's like built-up awkwardness in your own mind." I pause, feeling my throat get lumpy. "I mean, what was the point in me getting so upset just when my mom was depressed? It didn't make anything better. It didn't help her feel better AT ALL. It made everything worse!" I feel myself screaming now and try to calm down. "There's no point in dwelling on bad stuff, I promise you."

She shakes her head then, and tears start trickling

down her cheeks. "You don't get it. You can't just, like, pretend things are fine, and ignore what's going on! You can't just, like, make the script you've written in your mind into reality, Natty." She sniffles. "Forget it. I'll talk to you later."

She hangs up before I have a chance to say goodbye. I know I don't get it, and I know I should try harder to get it, but right now, I really have to focus on other things.

Gracie will be okay. Gracie is always okay.

From: Natty Blaken
To: Miller Creek Pep Squad
Subject: REMINDER Girls Volleyball Game TOMORROW!

Hi, Peppy People!

Just a reminder we have a bonus event tomorrow after school. Come straight to the gym. Bring all of your homemade signs. I'll have the pompoms. Be prepared to DANCE YOUR HEARTS OUT! Don't forget to start strong with the air-trumpet part! 😀

Forever peppy,

Natty J. Blaken

The next day is Grandma Becomes a School Lunch Caterer day and our last event before the pep rally so I wake up way before my alarm, so excited I can't possibly keep my eyes closed and stay in bed for another second.

I run down the stairs and Grandma's making cheesy eggs while labeling all the brown paper lunch bags at the same time. I know it's so much work, but I also think she was kind of made for this moment.

"Grandma! The kitchen smells so good!"

"I know, Natty! I made homemade chocolate chip scones, too."

Dad comes down to the kitchen a few minutes later—all freshly shaven with an ironed shirt on.

"Dad, you look so awake! So refreshed!" I pour a cup of orange juice for him and for me, and then pass one to him. "Are you going somewhere or something?"

"No, just a regular workday at the dining room table." He smiles.

"Natty, how are you going to be able to carry these lunches on the bus?" Grandma asks.

I realize right then that I hadn't thought of that. "Hmmm."

"I'll drive you," Dad says. "I've, um, been wanting to talk to you about something."

"Really?" My heart perks up a little because my dad and I haven't spent any time alone together since we moved to Miller Creek. Truthfully, we were never a dad/

daughter duo that really hung out one-on-one, though. It was always the three of us: Dad, Mom, and me. That's kind of how it works when you're an only child.

It *would* be hard to take all the lunches on the bus, and a ride with Dad to talk, just the two of us, feels like a good thing.

I put all the brown lunch bags in a giant shopping bag, take my final sip of orange juice, and then clear my plate. "Ready to go, Dad?"

"Yup, meet me in the car."

"Thank you again for making all these lunches, Grandma."

"Oh, Natty, it's nothing." She sniffles a little and then looks at me all sympathetic and sad. "I want to do whatever I can to make life good for you."

"Life is great for me, Grandma!"

"Natty." She tips her head to the side a little, kind of a *come on, be real* expression. "You sleep on an old futon in an attic and had to leave your friends and the whole community you loved so much and come to this town that is not what it used to be. We don't even have a synagogue for your bat mitzvah yet and—"

"Grandma, stop," I interrupt her. "I get to live with my grandparents and really know you both in a different way. The synagogue thing will work out, and I'm building a new community here! I've met really nice kids and this pep squad is soooo fun! People are really getting into it."

"Okay." She sighs. "Well, I love you. So that's something."

"That's everything!" I shriek, and we hug, and then I get into the car and yell out "thank you" to Grandma three more times through the open window.

I wonder why she got so emotional. Sure, she made a bunch of lunches, but I didn't expect her to feel so many feelings all at once.

"So, what did you want to talk about, Dad?" I ask once my seat belt is buckled.

He clears his throat. "Well, um, I just sort of wanted to see how you're settling in here. . . ."

"Settling in great; already settled, actually, and loving it," I answer.

"Mmm-hmm," he replies.

"What about you?" I ask. "It seems like you're doing much better than when we originally got here, so yay for that!" I clap and turn the music down a little bit. "Grandma said you ended your medical leave from work early and you can work remotely forever? So that's amazing!"

"I am, yeah. I'm feeling much better, happy to be back to work, for sure. And yes, I was hesitant about coming back here. I'm sure you can tell the town is extremely depressed since the shoe manufacturers closed. It's a huge struggle for everyone." He pauses. "I spent my whole childhood wanting to leave, but now that I'm back I can see some of the positives."

"A lot of positives," I add. "I know the economy is struggling, but aside from that, Miller Creek has a lot to offer."

"It has potential," Dad replies like he's putting an end to this sort of strange debate we found ourselves in. "Is it weird for you to be the only Jewish kid? I know that's a huge change from Willets, and it wasn't always like that here. There used to be more of us. . . ."

"Yeah, but it's okay. I'm fine with it. Makes me stand out." I smile and look over at him, but he doesn't notice. His hands are tight on the wheel, and he's staring directly at the road in front of him.

We're quiet then and I start to think that's the end of what he wanted to discuss. I look out the window at all the buildings with For Rent signs and dilapidated houses and the movie theater that no longer shows movies and the tennis courts without nets outside the recreation center that also needs a paint job and doesn't appear to be open at all anymore.

"You can see yourself staying here?" he asks. He clears his throat again and I start to realize this talk is actually really hard for him. I guess he was never the one who brought up the tough subjects. That was Mom. And even when she did, he didn't always want to get into it.

Thinking about it now, maybe she felt like leaving was the only way to really change things up, to get us (or Dad, really) to understand how sad she was feeling.

"Yeah, I mean, we need Mom to come, and I'm working

on that, so . . . it'll be great when she does come. It's great now, but you know what I mean—it'll be the best when she gets here." I sit back in my seat and turn on the warmer since it's suddenly freezing in this car. My thoughts are spiraling around my brain so fast I'm having trouble figuring out what I'm saying.

"Well, Natty, about that." He pauses. "You can't really control it."

"I know I can't control it, but I can show her how great it is, and she won't want to miss something that amazing." I turn off the music now because, even though it's soothing James Taylor, it's somehow giving me a headache so early in the morning.

"Natty, it's just—" He stops talking and then starts again. "It's just, people may see it differently."

"What people? And anyway, that's because people focus on the negative! So stop. We totally got way too negative with Mom last year. It made everything worse." I feel myself raising my voice a little, the way I did with Gracie on FaceTime last night, and I take a few deep breaths to calm myself down. "It's all good, Dad. It's all gonna be good and stay good and then eventually be great. I mean it is great now, but *you* have to see it as great!" We turn into the side parking lot at school, and I force the tears to stay back. Good thing we've run out of time for this discussion.

I hop out of the car and grab the bag of lunches and my

backpack and thank my dad for the ride.

"You're welcome, Natty. Love you."

I head inside, that tickly conversation still swirling around in my head, and the tears sort of piling up behind my eyeballs. I'm not totally sure he said what he had planned to say, but it doesn't matter. I have lunches for people and the sun is shining and it's going to be a great day!

"Yo, Lunch Girl!" Wade yells to me from down the hall as soon as I pass the vending machine. "Excited for our gourmet eats today!"

"You should be excited." I smile and yell back. "It's all really, really good."

Soon the rest of the lunch table crew meets me at my locker, and I hand out all the bags. Grandma wrote each of their names on them, following the list I made for her.

Mack comes by a minute later. Her hair is unbrushed, and she's wearing her stained green sweatshirt again. Her eyes are still half-closed.

"Mack!" I squeal. "You're here. I have your lunch!"

"Natty, no. Too loud. Too early. So tired." She plops herself down on the floor and makes a pillow out of her backpack the way she always does lately.

I sit down next to her and try to do all I can to be a comforting, kind friend. "What's going on? Are you feeling sick?"

"No, just tired. We have the most annoying toddler

next door who screams about everything." She squeezes her eyes shut even tighter. "It's really so loud and so terrible."

"Wow. Yeah."

"The walls are so thin. It's like the monster literally lives with us."

"Well, rest up now—you have time for a ten-minute power nap and they say that's actually the perfect length. You'll feel as if you slept for nine hours."

"Whatever you say, Natty," she groans.

I'm realizing she kinda says this a lot, and I try not to laugh about that. I lean back against the locker and text Grandma that everyone is so excited for her lunches.

When the bell rings, I drag Mack up from the floor and sort of pull her down the hallway with me until we get to Advisory.

As soon as we walk in the door, I'm overwhelmed with a brilliant idea, and I need to ask Ms. Lamlot about it right away.

She's at her desk organizing some papers.

"Ms. Lamlot, can I ask you a question? Oh, and first of all, good morning!"

She looks up at me and smiles and says, "Good morning, Natty!"

I glance over at her desk and there's a card envelope, like a greeting card you'd get for an anniversary or a birthday. It's canary yellow and it says, "Gwen," on the front. And I swear it's my dad's handwriting. It has to be. I know that handwriting like I know my own.

"Can I help you with something?" she asks, and I realize I was totally not paying attention to whatever she said before that.

"Oh, um, yeah." I shuffle my feet a little and stumble getting more words to come out of my mouth. "I was wondering if we could spend Advisory making signs for the pep rally. I know not everyone is part of the squad, but it would be great if as many students as possible had signs to encourage cheering and school spirit and stuff. I really want this to be a full-community kind of thing."

"What a great idea! I don't see why not." She sits back in her chair and gazes out the window and then looks back at me. "Why don't you announce it to the class after our morning stretches?"

"Great! I will. I'm going to run to the art room and grab supplies. Be right back!"

When I get back to Advisory, I put the poster board and markers down at the front of the classroom and then go to my seat. Mack is at the desk next to mine, her head resting on her jacket, her mouth open, drool dripping from her lips. Ew.

"Mack," I say. "Wake up."

"Noooo. I was having this dream where I won a trip to Hawaii, and you yanked me out of it, Natty. Take me back, take me back," she whines.

"Shhh." I shake my head. "It's okay."

Ms. Lamlot leads us in some morning stretches and then she calls me up to make my announcement.

"Hello, lovely Advisory classmates!" I say. "Happy Friday! We are having the FIRST-EVER Miller Creek Junior High School pep rally in a little under two weeks, and we get to miss the last period of the day! We have an *aaaahmazing* pep squad. But you can all participate! I've scrounged up some poster board and markers from the art room, and we're all going to make signs to show our school spirit!"

"Is this for real?" one of the boys in the back asks. I can't tell which one.

"Yes! It is for real!" I shout. "And it is great! Come on, grab a poster board, grab a marker, write some fun stuff. Let's go!"

"Nattyyyyy," Mack groans. "I told you I was so tired, and you're making us do arts and crafts. You are the wooorsstt."

"Come on, Mack, a little drawing can't be too taxing on you, especially since you love to doodle!"

It takes everyone a few moments to get up, but they eventually grab the stuff and start making signs. Some just say, "CHEER NOW!" or "GO, TEAM!" or "MILLER CREEK IS A TOWN," but there are others that say, "YAY, MILLER CREEK JUNIOR HIGH!" and "MILLER CREEK FROGS ARE

THE BEST!" and "WE LOVE MILLER CREEK JUNIOR HIGH SCHOOL!"

In the end, I'm not sure it matters so much what they say, just that there are colorful signs to be held up and people there in the bleachers holding the colorful signs.

Baby steps. It's all about baby steps.

When the bell rings before lunch, I grab Mack's hand. "Come on, you're coming to eat lunch with me today."

"What? No. Natty! That wasn't part of the deal."

"Well, it is now. I brought you homemade lunch. Now sit with me."

"With those delinquents? No. I can't believe you even speak to them, let alone make them lunch." She motions with her hand to get me to move back. "You don't even know what they've done to me!"

"Yeah, because you won't tell me! And they're part of the pep squad! They're not delinquents. They had one misstep. Now come on!" I grab her hand again, a little more forcefully and pull her to the cafeteria.

"I am regretting every single thing I've ever done or said in regard to you," Mack says through clenched teeth. "You are a demon."

I ignore her and keep hustling toward the cafeteria. She groans the whole way.

We get to the table and all the kids are there: Luna and

Wade and Tape and Braid.

"Oh, Lunch Girl! You're here!" Wade gives me two thumbs-up. "This lunch is *so* good!"

Tape shakes her head. "For real, Lunch Girl. This is quality. And I can't believe you followed through!"

"Well, duh. Of course, I followed through!"

"Holy shiiivers," Braid says. "This is beyond. Look how she wrapped my tuna sandwich. Is this wax paper?"

"Yup." I beam.

"This is professional looking, like a real deli," Wade adds. "Wow, Lunch Girl." He nods and stares at me. "Wow, thank you."

"Natty! This is DELISH." Luna does a teeny, tiny dance in her seat. "Your grandma should definitely be a caterer."

"Oh lord, I can't watch this," Mack says. She leaves her bag on the table and runs out of the cafeteria.

"That girl is a lost cause," Braid says after a bite of turkey wrap. "Truly miserable since kindergarten. Like, didn't even get excited when the parachute came out in gym class, and we allllll got excited for that!"

"Really?" I ask. "Parachutes rule!"

"They do rule! Why are we too old for parachutes?" Wade ponders for a moment, and then he pats the chair next to him. "Why are you still standing? Sit down, Lunch Girl. You need to eat, too!"

I smile. "I need to go find Mack."

I take Mack's lunch bag and mine, too, and start walking away.

"Suit yourself," Wade says. "And thanks again, Lunch Girl."

"Yeah, thanks," they all mumble, food in their mouths.

"Natty, I'll come find you in a minute!" Luna yells when I'm already a little bit of a distance from the table. "When I'm done eating!"

I walk around school, feeling so happy that they all love their lunches, while worrying about Mack at the same time. Finally, I find her in the little vestibule outside the gym.

"Here's your lunch. Just eat it. I know you're hungry and you're Freddy the Frog, so you need the sustenance for the volleyball game later."

"Go away, Natty. I'm so done with you."

I lean back against the wall and fold my arms over my chest. I'm ready to listen to whatever she has to say. "How come?"

"Because you're so annoying, because you pretend things are great when they suck, because somehow I decided I should be a mascot and now I'm stuck with it." She pauses and glares at me. "Should I go on?"

"Sure. If you want to. Let it out. Let it all out."

She turns away from me and spreads her legs out so they take up the full length of the step she's sitting on.

"That's the thing, though, you don't really want me to let it all out. It's just a thing you've heard someone say once, but you don't believe it; you don't want anyone to let anything out! You want everyone to just be happy even if things are so so freakin' terrible!"

"That's not true." I shake my head, feeling like the pile of tears from before is about to pour out of my eyes.

"It is true. Just go away. Thanks for lunch." She stretches out her legs in front of her. "I'll be at the game today and then the pep rally but that's it. After that, Freddy the Frog is dead."

"Well, I'm glad Freddy will be there today. See you later."

I leave her sitting there, but when she's not looking, I peer in through the little glass window at the top of the door.

I see her smiling as she unwraps her sandwich and as she rips open the bag of kettle chips.

By the time I leave Mack, there are only ten minutes left of lunch, so I take my bag into the library and sit at one of the study desks.

Brie and apple and a tiny bit of honey mustard—my favorite.

I think about how Grandma made six different lunches today, how they all were presented so beautifully, it really would seem that she's a professional caterer. I bet she never expected to be doing this when she was seventy-six years old. I bet she never expected her son and granddaughter would come to live with her either. But she rolls with it. She smiles through it.

There is so much happiness around us and I don't understand why Mack can't see that.

All I know is, I'm going to keep working on her.

24

IT'S AMAZING WHAT A FEW homemade lunches can do to a pep squad! Well, part of a pep squad. Grandma didn't make the lunches for Terra, Kingsley, and Rowan or Lance and his friends, but my lunch table crew seems way more energetic than usual!

"Okay, everyone, this is our last thing before the pep rally, so consider it like a dress rehearsal. Let's really crush our routine. Remember to be in sync as we air-trumpet out; don't forget the face display and the finger shaking. ALL OF IT WILL BE AWESOME."

"Lunch Girl, cheer down a little, this is still a little more intense than I have energy for," Braid says.

"LOL, cheer down." I smile. "Good one, Braid."

"Okay, everyone, just go with it," Luna says, smiling at me. "At the last event, she suggested we carry the pom-poms in our armpits, so this is an improvement. But no matter what—she's awesome."

"Aw, Luna." I put an arm over her shoulders.

"Wait, so what actually happens at the pep rally?" Kingsley sing-song asks. "I don't get it. Like, we do our routine and then?"

"All the different sports teams will come out, we'll introduce each player, we'll blast music, and everyone will dance around. The mayor will speak. . . . We'll do our routine and cheer. It's like a half-hour event at the end of the day."

"Ahhh." Kingsley nods. "I thought it was wayyyy longer."

"Me, too," Rowan adds.

"Um, like, no offense, though, but there are like two people here from our team. Where is everyone? And the net is sort of, like, falling over," Kingsley says. "So can they even play like this? I don't get it."

I look around and she's right. Thankfully the speakers are set up today, but most of the team isn't here, and there's barely anyone on the indoor bleachers to watch the game.

Across the gym I see the other team is here—a school called Wellnock Junior High. Wellnock sounds familiar; I think that's where Grandma said the synagogue is. All their players are warming up and seem excited to play. But I have no idea where the Miller Creek team is!

I walk over to one of the Miller Creek players. I think she's in eighth grade. "Hiiii, I'm Natty. I'm in charge of the pep squad. Are we still waiting for the rest of the team or—?"

"Oh yeah, we only have, like, six players to begin with and most won't show up. Our coach has a stomach bug—that's what I heard anyway—so we'll prob forfeit again."

"Really?" My heart sinks to my feet. We have the whole pep squad here and they're actually energized (and some are well fed) and we're all set with our awesome routine, and now the team we're cheering for is missing?

"Yeah, girl, sorry. You can still, like, do your dance and stuff? I saw it at the boys soccer game. It was actually pretty good." She shrugs.

Well, at least there's that! And the boys soccer game was probably our worst performance. We barely knew the routine!

We wait a few more minutes, and then the coach from the other team says that they're going to need to get started.

"Don't worry; we'll get everyone fired up!"

"Um, there's really no one here. . . ." He looks toward the bleachers.

"It's okay! You're here! I'm here!"

I get the squad ready, make sure the speakers are on, "Cheerleader" starts, and we air trumpet out onto the gym floor.

All of us are coordinated—the windmill, side steps, the claps, emoji hands, finger shaking, all of it. We are all doing it together, moving together, smiling together. No doubt this is the best we've ever done it!

Mack comes out as Freddy, dances around; we all clap for her.

After the routine, we do our back-and-forth Miller Creek/Go, Frogs cheer and it's absolutely, positively perfect. Energetic! Excited! Everything you'd want a pep squad to be!

We finish cheering and I look out into the bleachers. Six people are clapping and then the three players from our volleyball team join in, too, and even the other school's team starts cheering for us. It's a little half-hearted feeling, but I guess they're trying.

"So, um, that was great, but I think we need to cancel this game," the Wellnock coach says quietly to me. "According to the Culver County Sports Manual, this is a win for us. If one team fails to supply the players and the coach, the other team wins."

A few minutes later, the volleyball players file out and the pep squad hangs on the bleachers for a bit.

"Guys, that was amazing!" I shout. "Seriously the best. Did you feel how great we did?"

"Um, no offense, Natty, but no one was here to even see it," Rowan replies. "The game got canceled and our team didn't even show up. It doesn't matter if it was amazing."

"It matters because it was our rehearsal for the pep rally and we crushed it!" I scream. "WE TOTALLY CRUSHED IT."

"Don't listen to her," Mack says to everyone, through the Freddy the Frog head. "She'll turn anything positive. Just ignore her."

"Well, I'm ignoring *that*!" I laugh. "Seriously, great job today, squad."

"We did crush it," Lance says to the group, standing up and clapping, like he's suddenly in charge. I can't say I hate it, though. "Honestly. We're good at this! And listen, before everyone leaves, I actually have another idea for a dance, routine, whatever you want to call it," he says.

"You do?" Marcus asks, shocked sounding, fully cracking up. "I gotta see this."

"I do, and it's going to Blow. Your. Minds." Lance hops down from the bleachers and stands in front, facing all of us. "You know the song, 'Sweet Caroline,' by legend Neil Diamond?"

"Um, yes!" Wade yells from the row behind me. "My grandma has an actual crush on Neil Diamond, but anyway." He laughs. "Go on. . . ."

"Sooooo I basically think it's a brilliant song, and so many sports teams use it so I can't exactly say it's my idea, but we can change the 'bum-bum-bum' to 'Mil-ler Creek' and it fits legit amazing." He puts his hands on his hips. "We were all BORN TO DO THIS SONG, PEOPLE!"

"OMG, LANCE!" I scream. "We need to do this. NEED TO. Do you want to put the music on or should I?"

Mack shakes her head. "Oh boy. Here we go." But she's smiling the teeniest, itty-bitty smile and I can tell even Mack is having fun right now.

Lance puts on the song and he demonstrates the moves we should do. Basically swaying our arms above our heads and snapping, dancing with our arms, some side steps. "See, nothing too complicated!" he yells over the music.

And then when the "bum-bum-bum" part comes he motions to us and we all yell, "MIL-LER CREEK!" It feels so fun and peppy that we literally all start laughing after that.

"Come try this with me!" Lance yells to everyone, and of course there are a bunch of groans, but then the whole squad gets up and joins him, and we follow along with the sways and the snaps and the side steps. There are even some squats with side leg kicks and maybe he's making this up as we go along, but it's great.

"I'm recording so we'll remember what to do," Luna whispers as she holds up her phone and tries to do the moves at the same time.

"Who is this kid?" Terra mouths to me, while snapping. "He's honestly so cute, right?"

I nod. I kinda thought I was the only one who secretly thought that. Guess not.

The song ends, Lance puts his phone back in his pocket, and turns to me. "So? You like it?"

"Um, like?" I shriek. "Hello! Love!"

"Natty!" Terra hits me on the arm and then covers her mouth, like she's regretting drawing attention to the fact that I just said "love" when talking about a Lance thing.

Flustered, I say, "I mean, I love the song, duh."

Terra shakes her head and looks over at Mack, and then Mack does the same head shake, and they both start laughing, and it's a moment where it's pretty obvious they're connecting over how silly I can be at times, but I don't care! They're connecting. For real. Right now. It's happening!

"Perfect way to end the pep rally, right?" Lance says. "I mean, I'm even shocked myself that I thought of it and decided to bring it up today, but it just felt like something we had to do."

Marcus, Chris, and Trey burst into hysterics at that point, but I can tell they're impressed with their friend. Even if it's just a little bit.

"Yes! Round of applause for Lance!" I clap, and motion for everyone to join with me. "Thank you SO much!"

We all hang out a little bit longer and when everyone leaves the gym, I stay back to make sure the pom-poms and posters are put away. I walk home and think about what a win today was!

Grandma made lunches and everyone loved
them.
Our routine was literally perfect at the volleyball
game.
My whole Advisory made posters for the pep rally.
Lance came up with a whole routine on his own.
I may have the tiniest itty-bitty baby crush on
Lance? Maybe?

I mean, those are five huge-deal, big things. I refuse to get discouraged just because the volleyball game didn't actually happen.

We totally spread joy while practicing, connecting as a squad, and getting ready for the pep rally at the same time.

All around a huge win.

25

THE REST OF THE WEEK flies by. There's Grandma's catering that everyone loves and daily lunchtime practices with Terra and Luna, plus a general sense that something good is coming, that I'm on a path to everything falling perfectly into place.

On Friday, I go to my locker to get the lunches and take them to the cafeteria to hand out because I didn't see everyone in the morning.

I quickly check my phone and find a text from my mom that makes my stomach sink.

Mom: Call me when you can.

I don't think anyone ever wants to get a text like that, especially not me and especially not from my mom, but I push it aside for now. I just don't have time to think about it.

After all the other lunches are handed out, I take mine and Luna's with me and go meet Terra and Luna in the gym for a little lunchtime practice.

"Hey, um, would it be crazy if I came with you?" Mack asks, catching up to me as I head out of the cafeteria. "I, just, um want to make sure I have the routine totally down and, like, know exactly when to come in as Freddy. And yeah, I mean, Luna and Terra have been nicer to me lately, so . . . I was just wondering."

"Mack! Of course! Come! I've been hoping you'd ask, but I didn't want to force you and you know how you can get. . . ." I widen my eyes.

"Don't make this a huge thing, Natty."

"Of course. Definitely not a huge thing."

"You say 'of course' a lot. Did you know that?" Mack asks.

I shrug. "Of course."

She swats my arm with hers, and we walk quietly the rest of the way to the gym.

"Oh my god, everyone has one of these fancy lunches except me," Terra says when we walk in. "I don't get it. Natty. What do I have to do to get your grandma to make *me* lunch?"

Laughing, I say, "I'll add you to the list."

We turn on the music and start with our air trumpet, and we try to make it look super tight, each step exactly in sync with the others, and the more we practice, the better it is. Mack joins in, practicing, too, even though she's not in her Freddy costume and she doesn't usually do this part.

Luna stops abruptly and says, "Wait, what if no one shows for this pep rally? Like most of the volleyball team bailed on *their own* game. You probably know this by now, but people kinda don't show up for stuff here." She pauses. "What do we do if no one comes?"

I shake my head. "Not possible. That's why it's scheduled during the actual school day. It's last period, so everyone comes as a class. It's, like, required. I mean, it *is* required. They're gonna take attendance and stuff."

"You think of everything, Natty," Luna replies.

I smile and we go back to practicing, the "Cheerleader" one and even the "Sweet Caroline" one that Lance came up with. We watch the video of it three times, and my face seems to get hotter each time we see it.

"He's kinda cute, right?" I say finally, at the end of our third viewing.

"OMG! I knew it! I knew you liked him," Luna shrieks.

"Shhh!" I swat her arm. "I'm just asking!"

"Yes. The answer is yes," Terra replies. "He is cute. Very, very cute."

We're on the bleachers, on a water break, discussing Lance for probably too long, when I hear my phone ringing.

It's Gracie.

We're not even supposed to have phones out during the day, and I can't believe I forgot to leave it in my locker, and I especially can't believe I forgot to put it on Silent.

"Oh my god, Natty, I am sooo relieved you answered," she says. "I didn't think you'd have your phone on. We're at lunch now, and literally they're all icing me out. Literally ignoring me at the table. Nisha is the only one acting normal." She stops talking and it sounds like she's crying, but there's random banging in the background and it's really hard to hear. "I had to sneak to the bathroom to call you. I'm freaking out."

"Wait, what, slow down," I say, and take her off speaker phone.

"I think they honestly don't want to be my friends anymore and I don't even know where to go and what to do and where to sit." She pauses. "I just snuck out of lunch and I'm probably going to get in so much trouble, but I'm so upset right now."

"I'm probably gonna get in trouble, too," I say. "Um, let me think."

"Natty, this is so bad." She sobs. "I don't get it. I didn't do anything."

I hesitate, but then I say, "You know what, Gracie? I feel like this is a blessing. These people are terrible, and The Core moms were mean to my mom, and then I felt like I couldn't be real with The Core, and then my mom left, and you were the only one who even cared, they all ignored me, and now they're being mean to you! It's a sign from the universe that you need to branch out and find other friends."

"Natty? What?" She pauses. "That's the answer? It's not that easy. I can't just find other friends."

"Gracie, you're strong, and you're gonna get through this! Hold your head high. I keep telling you, act like you don't care, and they can't get to you!" I pause. "It's all in your attitude! The vibes you put out make a huge difference."

She's silent then and doesn't respond and I see some teachers pacing by the side of the gym door. My stomach twists into a pretzel again. Gracie sounds so sad, and I'm worried I'll get caught with my phone. And the text from my mom is lingering in the back of my mind, impossible to not think about. I was just having so much fun with Terra, Luna, and Mack, but now I feel like I'm going to pass out.

"Gracie, I gotta go, teachers are coming. Call you later. Bye."

I end the call and put my phone on Silent and back in my bag.

"Um, what was that?" Terra asks me, putting her hair up in a high ponytail.

"My best friend, Gracie, from my old town, she's going through friend drama," I explain, and then go to turn the music back on so we can go through the routine again. "I got so stressed I'd get in trouble for being on the phone at school."

Terra looks at me. "Sounds like she's going through a big thing, and you kinda like told her to just move on."

"Hello! This is what I've been saying!" Mack yells. "Thank you."

"But it doesn't make sense to dwell on it. The Core's just not that great," I explain. "She'll find other friends. . . ."

"It's not that easy," Mack says, and then makes a face like she's regretting saying that. "I mean, like, anyway, never mind."

They shrug and sort of sigh like they realize they're not getting through to me. We go back to practicing, but my stomach hurts so much, I need to stop three times and take a break and sit down on the bleachers. I don't even feel like eating my lunch.

For the rest of the day, I'm all twisted up from the Gracie call and the reactions to it, plus that text from my mom that I've been trying to ignore.

That night after dinner, I FaceTime Gracie but she doesn't answer. I make three more posters for the pep rally even though we probably have more than enough. But someone in the crowd may need one.

CLAP YOUR HANDS FOR MILLER CREEK!

MILLER CREEK, WE 🖤 YOU!

SHOW SOME LOVE FOR MILLER CREEK!

Everyone has been doing great with making posters, especially the lunch table crew, which makes sense since I guess they really like to draw on stuff.

After that, I realize I can't ignore my mom's text anymore. I have to call her back and hear what she's going to say. I hope it's that she booked a room at the new inn and that we're having a sleepover and then fancy breakfast the next morning with all of our food on a silver platter and our orange juice in a glass carafe. I hope she's going to say she's planning to move here with us, and she'll be at the pep rally, and she's recovered and ready to start fresh.

"Hi, Mom," I say, right after her hello. "How are you? Everything is amazing here! We have sooo many posters for the pep rally, and you're not going to believe how amazing our routines are. Seriously, this is the best thing I've ever been part of. I CANNOT wait for you to see it all!"

"Natty, yeah, about that . . ."

"Also, I just reallllly want to see *you*." I pause. "And if you stay through Saturday, we can go to services together in Wellnock. Get this—the synagogue there is called Congregation Yad B'Yad, like hand in hand. That song you love!" I shriek.

There's silence on the phone then, and my mom finally says, "Natty, that all sounds so good." She pauses for a really long time, and I start to worry she's passed out or something. "But I'm not feeling up to making the trip yet. And I am truly so sorry. I know how hard you've been working, and the pep rally is a big event, and the synagogue sounds lovely, and I'm grateful to Grandma for finding it. I just don't know when I'll be able to make it to Miller Creek. . . ."

"Well, it's only Friday. The pep rally is Monday so you can still change your mind, last minute. . . . You're not that far, and if your car is still in the shop, there are so many buses. . . ." My voice trails off.

"I'm sorry, Natty. I love you. I miss you. I wish that things were different."

"There's still so much good stuff, though, Mom." My words catch in my throat. I snuggle up under my blanket. "Really. I mean, I'm making all these new friends, and Dad seems good, and it's actually great to live with Grandma and Grandpa."

"That's great to hear, Natty. Really."

"So then can't you just—" I hesitate. "Can't you just be happy?"

She sniffles then, and I know she's crying, and I swallow hard and then swallow again because I refuse to cry, too.

I say, "I just want you to see all the good things.

They're all there! Really they are." I curl into a ball on my bed. "Just think about coming to see the pep rally, K? You don't need to decide today." I pause. "But I need to go now, and um, make some more posters. Love you, Mom."

"Love you, too, Natty-girl."

I stare up at my slanted attic ceiling and a little bit later, I hear the squeak of the screen door downstairs as Dad comes into the house.

I close my eyes and go to sleep. I can't think about anything else today. I just need to rest. Things will be clearer in the morning.

They always are.

26

I SPEND THE WEEKEND PRACTICING the routines in front of the full-length mirror in the attic, emailing the mayor to confirm he's coming, trying not to get all twisted up worrying about my mom and her flaky plans to visit, and putting up more flyers around town with Terra and Luna.

Then on Monday morning, Pep Rally Day, the three of us get to school early to hang up more pep rally signs all over the building.

We hang up our last flyer, outside the third-floor bathroom, and I say, "Remember the squad got permission to leave class fifteen minutes early to meet all the teams in the gym," I remind them.

"Natty! We know!" Terra shakes her head. "You've told us a million times!"

"Yeah, girl, plus you think I'd ever forget the chance to leave class early?" Luna laughs. "No way."

After that, time seems to go in slow motion all day, but I finally walk out of my math classroom after eighth period feeling so fizzy and excited I think I'd be able to jump up and touch the ceiling right now. I know my mom said she wasn't gonna come, but there's still a teeny, tiny corner of my brain where I think she may actually show up and surprise me and I'll look out into the bleachers and see her there, sitting next to my dad, and smiling.

Mack and I leave math together to go straight to the single-stall bathroom on the second floor. I'm going to guard the door while she gets into the Freddy the Frog costume and then we'll meet the rest of the squad in the gym.

"Ready?" I ask when we're in the hallway. "I am soooo excited!"

"Uh, Natty," she says, looking through the doorway of an empty classroom.

"Yeah?"

"Look outside the school. Right now." She pauses. "Do you see what's happening?"

We walk through the classroom and stare through the window at rows of teachers, I guess from all the schools in the district, holding up signs and walking back and forth.

"I have no idea what's happening. I'm really confused." My heart pounds.

Mack crinkles her eyes and turns to face me. "Looks like they're on strike? I think?"

"Now? Today? But the pep rally is right now. That's why the school day ended early, so there's time for everyone to get outside. That's how we planned it. You need to be Freddy the Frog. I need to find the rest of the squad. It's on the community calendar. The mayor is coming!"

"Natty." She grabs my arm. "Get ahold of yourself. I don't think it's happening. The teachers are on strike!" We start to hear so much noise in the hallway. "I think everyone is leaving! No one is coming. There's no pep rally."

I shake my head. "No, no, no. This has to be a misunderstanding. It can still happen. We can do it without the teachers. We've done everything this whole time without Mr. Woodson!"

An announcement comes over the loudspeaker a second later. "Students, please head to your buses. The pep rally has been canceled. Please exit the building immediately."

"I don't understand. I need to figure this out." I rush away and walk into the main office and Sheila is sitting there, at her desk, working on a thick book of Sudoku.

I say out of breath, "What's happening? The pep rally was supposed to be today. Can you page Mr. Woodson?"

"Sorry, dearie." She doesn't look up from the book. "You heard the announcement. I shouldn't even still be here."

My heart thumps out of control, so loud I hear it in my throat.

No no no no no. This isn't right. This can't be right. Ms. Lamlot didn't say anything about this when we made the signs in Advisory; Mr. Woodson didn't mention a single thing.

I quickly scroll through my email to see if Mayor Giff said anything when he wrote me back last week.

From: Mayor Giff
To: Natty Blaken
Subject: RE: Pep Rally

> **Dear Natty,**
> **I'd be honored to announce the event.**
> **Best wishes,**
> **Mayor Giff**

Nothing at all! He was planning to be here! He may even be on his way!

I walk back into the hallway, brushing the sweat off my forehead with the sleeve of my sweatshirt. I'll find the pep squad—Terra, Kingsley, Rowan, Luna and the lunch crew, Lance and his friends, and Mack, of course—and maybe we can still do something. Lance's "Sweet Caroline" routine at least! We can cheer and people can hold posters, and we'll drag as many kids out there as we can, and yeah, maybe it's weird with teachers picketing out front, but we can do it.

"Lunch Girl, what is happening?" Braid asks me. The lunch table crew is gathered around my locker. "I was set to be peppy, thanks to Grandma's lunches."

Luna lifts her eyebrows. "I think Braid really means that this time."

"I don't know what's happening," I reply, my stomach twisting around and around. I breathe in deeply, afraid I might throw up right here. "Something about a strike?"

"Do we need to stay?" Tape asks me.

"I don't know. Try to, I guess?"

I keep walking down the hall, peeking my head into every classroom, hoping to find a teacher who can tell me what's going on.

"Oh my god, this is soooo crazy," Kingsley sing-song screams from a few feet away. "Natty, I think the pep rally is canceled. We may not have school all week!" she yells all the way down the hallway.

I freeze in my steps then and walk over to her. "Really?"

"Yeah, the teachers refuse to work or something," Rowan replies, not sounding fazed at all.

I swallow hard, feeling tears bubbling up in my chest somehow. "Just hang around, okay? Don't leave yet.

Maybe we can figure something out."

I have no idea where Terra is.

I start walking again, really fast, looking into each and every classroom. Students are scattered everywhere; most are just leaving the building. Even the janitor has abandoned his garbage can and mop. Whiteboards are left with writing all over them.

"Natty." Mack finds me again. She's wearing the bottom of her Freddy the Frog costume and holding the head. "I think we should go. Things feel eerie around here."

"I don't know what's going on." My words come out all shaky. The tears are trickling down my cheeks. I can't hide them at all now. I can't stop them. I feel completely powerless over my own body. "I don't understand this."

She gives me a confused look, like she's not sure why it's not making sense to me. "This happens sometimes. The teachers go on strike because their union doesn't really work and they never get raises or sick days and the budget keeps getting slashed every year. Do you know they have to pay for their own dry-erase markers?"

"They do?" I say. My words come out hoarse, thick puddles forming behind my eyeballs. My heart physically hurts. My skin is itchy all over like I'm breaking out in hives. *What is happening. What is happening. What is happening.*

Her voice turns quieter, softer. "I've been telling you it's pretty awful here. You still don't see this?"

I don't respond. I stand there frozen, staring at her, and then looking down the hall. Looking for what, I'm really not sure.

She sits down on the floor in front of one of the science labs. I peek in and there's the pile of broken microscopes in the corner. It's been there all year. I figured they were just waiting on a new shipment to come.

I sit down next to her and lean my head back against the wall. I close my eyes. The hallways are clearing out and it's quieter now. Even though they're outside on the sidewalk, all the way inside the school I hear the teachers yelling.

"We demand fair pay!" "Help us help the students!" "Help us help your kids!"

"Did you know most of the teachers have to drive for Uber and Lyft on weekends to pay their rent?" Mack asks me.

I shake my head.

She sits up straight and talks to me with her hands. Each word is angrier than the one before. "Did you know all of the eighth-grade history textbooks are held together with masking tape? We only have new ones in seventh grade because the teachers applied for some kind of grant."

I shake my head again. I sniffle and wipe the tears away with a tissue when Mack is looking the other way.

"Face reality, Natty. This isn't Willets or whatever it

was called where you used to live. No pep squad is going to help this place. We're doomed."

For the first time ever, I don't try to correct her. I don't say anything at all.

I close my eyes and sob.

I'm not sure how much time passes while Mack and I stay sitting there, but a little bit later, I feel a tap on my shoulder.

It's my dad.

"Natty, I've been trying to find you. Grandma, Grandpa, and I were in the car to come for the pep rally and then I got a call from Ms. Lamlot about the strike." He bites his bottom lip. "I'm so sorry this happened today. The teachers were trying to negotiate, but they didn't come to an agreement. I know how hard you've been working."

I nod. "Yeah."

My stomach twists again. I get that about-to-throw-up feeling. I want to get up and run to the bathroom, but I feel too worn out, too tired, too sad. I feel like I can't even move.

Ms. Lamlot comes up behind him a second later and they're just sort of standing over me in this awkward way like they're about to say something but haven't said it yet.

"Um, you've probably figured this out, but Gwen—I mean Ms. Lamlot"—he pauses after correcting himself—"and I have been spending time together."

Mack is still sitting next to me. She inches away a little and pretends to not be paying attention.

I nod. "Yeah, I guessed that."

"I know it's a little unusual for your dad to be friends with your teacher," Ms. Lamlot adds.

"Mmm-hmm."

Hold back the rest of your boulder-size tears, Natty, I tell myself. Don't cry again. Not here. Not in front of Ms. Lamlot. Not anywhere. It's all going to be okay. This won't last forever. Nothing does. All of this can be fixed. All of this can be great.

I tell myself all of the things I always do. But none of it works right now.

My stomach is twisted tighter than it's ever been before and I burst out into sobs right in the middle of the hallway. Splotchy, gigantic tears.

I open my mouth to talk and my words come out loud and harsh and cutting. "I hate this whole thing, Dad. I hate that we're here and I hate that Mom left and I hate that we're not in Willets. I hate that I tried so hard to start a pep squad and bring some joy to this place and even that failed!" I scream.

I scream so loud whoever is left in the hallway turns around.

I scream so loud it drowns out the sounds of the teachers picketing.

I scream so loud I give myself a headache.

"Whoa, Natty," Mack says, finally. "Get it, girl. I knew you had it in you. Let it out, girl. Let it out."

I turn to her. "Leave me alone, Mack. Don't talk to me!"

I get up then and hoist my backpack over my shoulders and walk away from all of them.

"Natty, please," I hear my dad say.

"No! Stop!" I scream. "Leave me alone!"

I ignore all of them. I don't need help. I don't want help. I don't know what I want but it's definitely not talking to any of them.

When I leave school, I walk past the parade of teachers on strike. There's Mr. Woodson with his hot-pink poster board with block letters that say, **"FAIR PAY NOW!"**

This is why he's been pretty much ignoring me. This is what all the meetings in his office were about. This is what he's been focusing on. This is why he completely abandoned the pep squad. This is why Wade and the others were talking about homeschooling that day.

I don't understand how Mr. Woodson could be in charge of running clubs, especially our brand-new one, and then just abandon us. How could he not care? How could Mom not care to see me or be here with me? And Dad not care to fix things with her and then just go and hang out with my teacher like it's totally normal.

None of it makes any sense at all. I don't understand why people do what they do.

I'm so lost in my own thoughts, I don't even realize

I've made it almost home.

I take my phone out of my pocket and hit the tab in my Favorites list to call my mom.

She answers on the third ring.

"Natty! How did the pep rally go?"

Flatly I say, "It didn't happen. The teachers went on strike."

"Really?"

"Yeah. Everything was for nothing, Mom."

"Oh, Natty. It wasn't for nothing. They'll reschedule it, I'm sure." She sighs, like she's going through the motions of what she has to say, but she doesn't really have time or even care so much.

"Yes, but it's still kind of sucky today, Mom. I've been trying to put a positive spin on everything because I thought that was how I could make you happy and prove to you that things were good." I hesitate to go on, but I do anyway. "And you know what? First of all, it didn't work. And second of all, not everything can be spun around in a positive way! Some things are just bad. And you're not coming back anyway. No matter what I do!"

"Natty, no . . ."

"Yes, Mom, yes. You walked out and I know you were sad and going through stuff, but now you don't even care to see me! You don't even miss me!"

There's silence then. The loudest silence I have ever, ever heard.

"Natty. That's not true. I do miss you. I know this is complicated. There's so much to process."

I want to throw my phone on the sidewalk and then smash it with my foot. She doesn't understand what I'm saying. Or she doesn't want to.

"I'm hanging up now, Mom. You don't understand me. You're not even hearing me!"

"I am hearing you. And I love you. Please know that. I just can't—"

I grumble a quick, "I have to go now," and then end the call.

I plop down on the steps, but I really don't want to be out here. I don't want to be anywhere. The sky is gray and cloudy, the leaves are falling off the trees, each house looks more dilapidated than the one next to it.

It's all sad and gloomy.

I don't know how I didn't see it until now. Maybe I wouldn't let myself.

I go inside the house finally and curl in a ball under the covers on my bed. I take out my phone and open FaceTime.

"Gracie," I say, sniffling as soon as she answers.

"Natty! Oh my god. What's wrong?" she asks, eyebrows crinkling. "You're crying."

"Everything fell apart," I say, curling myself into an even tighter ball. "The teachers went on strike and the pep rally didn't happen and my dad is hanging out with my Advisory teacher! It's all a mess." I sob and sob and sob and I can't get any more words out. My eyes are so filled with tears, I can barely see the screen.

"Natty, oh my goodness. I'm so sorry."

"I feel like every single thing has collapsed."

She waits a few seconds before responding. "Um, well, yeah. Now you kind of get how I've been feeling, I guess. . . ."

I sit up. "It's not the same, Gracie. Not to be rude, but you live in an awesome house and have amazing parents and the cutest little twin sisters, and you're smart and beautiful and . . ."

"Okay, stop. Never assume you know someone's life."

I stare at her through the screen.

"I need to go, Natty. I'm sorry you had such a bad day, but you're sounding so insensitive right now. I've reached out so many times to tell you how hard things are, and you haven't been there for me at all!" She hangs up before I even have a chance to reply.

Great.

Just add my best friend hating me onto the list of the absolute worst day in Natty history.

AFTER THAT, I CURL UP even tighter under the blanket, and I fall into such a deep sleep that I don't even change into my pajamas.

The next morning, I'm woken up by the nonstop buzzing of my phone on the night table.

Mack: NO SCHOOL TODAY! TEACHERS STILL ON STRIKE!

Me: I don't care. You woke me up.

Mack: This is the best news ever

Me: leave me alone.

Mack: Do I have the wrong number? Is this Natty? You don't sound like yourself.

Me: It's Natty

Me: Go away

Mack: You're freakin me out. I'm coming over.

I go downstairs to find something to eat because I'm starving from skipping dinner last night. I eat a banana in ten seconds and then devour three pieces of Grandma's crumb cake.

The doorbell rings a little while later, Grandma answers the door, and Mack comes rushing into the house. Soon she's standing directly over me. I'm under a blanket on Grandpa's recliner.

"Hi. Come outside. Now." Mack grabs my hand and pulls me up, takes my jacket off the coat tree, and within a minute, we're back in our favorite spot—my front steps.

I sit down and look over my shoulder and see Grandma peeking out from the dining room window. When our eyes meet, she quickly pretends to be doing something else.

"What's going on with you? What happened to 'good vibes only'?" Mack leans back and stretches her legs out in front of her.

It's freezing out here, like winter appeared all of a sudden even though it's still fall. I wish I was still inside under that blanket.

I don't answer. I don't have an answer. We sit there quietly and listen to the wind in the trees and the couple arguing on their front lawn three houses down the block. The air feels heavy between Mack and me, like all of our thoughts are spiraling around, and we don't know what to do with them.

The longer we sit here silently, the more awkward it is.

Finally, I can't take it anymore. I have to say something.

"It all stinks," I say finally. "I thought if I could do all the things and basically refuse to think of anything negative, I could convince my mom that things are great and convince her to move here and be with us, and it would actually all be great and she'd actually be happy."

"Mmmhmm. That's still the dumbest thing I've ever heard," Mack says, all matter-of-fact.

"Why are you here if you're only going to make me feel even worse than I already feel?" I ask.

"I don't know. I'm not trying to make you feel bad." She pauses. "I don't know what I'm doing."

I sigh. "Just stop, Mack. I get it. I understand what you're trying to do. You saw the issues all along and you were right and you want me to know that. People like to be right."

"Sorta. Kinda not really, though." She looks at me and exhales. "I kinda wish you had been right. . . ."

I look at her, finally. "I guess I need to accept that even the best pep squad can't fix the problems in the school and make people peppy if they don't want to be peppy, and I can't convince my mom to be here if she doesn't want to be."

"Yeah, pretty much, but also not totally," Mack says, and stands up and starts pacing slowly on the path leading up to the house. "Because here's the thing I did realize. Here's the thing you *made me realize*. Even though starting a pep squad was a pretty, uh, unique idea—we did all get into it in our own way. At least a little."

"Really?" My soul perks up when she says that.

"Yeah, totally. Terra and Luna actually became *friends* again. And they started being pretty nice to me, too. Which is honestly a miracle! Also, like, Luna and the rest of that crew have never done an extracurricular or cared about a school thing in their whole lives. And they actually showed up."

"Well, it was their punishment for the whole basketball court situation. . . ."

"Also, Natty, I've never had a friend like you before." She stops pacing then and looks at me. "And I know I give you a hard time and I know I'm not always nice—okay, I'm never nice—but I'm glad you're here. You *have* made things happier. You haven't solved all the problems of the town. But that's not your job. And it's also impossible."

"I don't think it's impossible. I still don't think it's impossible."

Mack laughs. "Ah, the Natty I know and love is still there. What a relief!"

I shake my head but eventually I start laughing, too, and it feels better to laugh than to feel as miserable as I was feeling before.

"Can you please tell me what happened between you

and Luna and them? And I guess how Terra, Kingsley, and Rowan fit into it, too? It's all kind of mysterious. . . . And—"

"Okay, stop with your commentary. I'll tell you." She looks at me, and I nod. "And then you have to tell me more about what happened with your mom and Willets and how you ended up in this trash heap of a town."

I tilt my head to the side, not really in the mood for all of that, but realizing I don't have much of a choice. "I think this calls for a heart-to-heart. We have a lot to talk about. Come in. I'll put out snacks, light one of my grandma's amazing WoodWick candles. . . ."

"I've never had a heart-to-heart," Mack says softly. "I don't even know what it is or how it works."

I try not to look at her like she's weird. "It's basically just a good talk. You don't have anything to worry about."

"I guess." She smiles, and even though she'd never admit it, I know she's excited about this.

We go inside and I put out a whole snack spread— grapes and string cheese, these fancy crackers Grandma loves, plus pretzels and hummus, slices of Grandma's crumb cake, and even a few of the dark chocolate squares Grandpa sneaks when he thinks no one is looking. It's early in the morning but a little dark chocolate is probably okay.

Grandma goes to the basement to start some laundry and Grandpa falls asleep reading the newspaper on the couch. Dad heads over to school for some impromptu parents meeting to discuss the strike.

"It feels so weird that it's the start of a school day and we're just home at the kitchen table, doesn't it?" I ask.

"Yeah. Feels great if you ask me. . . . Did your grandma make lunches for all of us thinking there'd be school today?"

"Good question. I'm not sure. I fell asleep in my clothes, didn't even eat dinner." I take a handful of grapes and finish chewing and then say, "So I guess I'll go first since you've never had a heart-to-heart before. . . ." I take a sip of water. "Basically, last year, my mom started to go down this really bad path, like super depressed, and then, like, all of the moms in the friend group started to turn away from her. Oh, I should back up. Basically all of my friends in my old town were daughters of my mom's friends. The moms all acted like teenagers, though—they called themselves The Core moms and had, like, a hashtag and stuff. It was so weird, and we called ourselves The Core. It sounds dumb."

Mack laughs. "Um, okay. Go on."

"So, like, basically it was all fake because when someone actually had a problem, they weren't there for them, and my mom kept feeling worse, and my dad and I tried to help, but we couldn't, really, and then we got really depressed, too, and then finally my mom decided she needed time to think about her life and stuff, and she went to Hawaii with some volunteer corps thing and we didn't know when she was coming back, and then my dad freaked out . . . and now we're here." I fold my hands on the table. "And I kinda thought if I could just prove to my mom that Miller Creek is great, she'd come and see that, and live with us here, and we could start fresh and all be happy, but . . ."

She interrupts me. "But it wasn't your job to do that, Natty. I'm sorry none of the adults in your life made that clear. . . ."

"Yeah, would have helped to kind of, like, been clued into that. And, um—"

Mack interrupts me again, but I don't really mind, for some reason. "And, also, you can't, like, *make* someone happy. . . ." She takes a pretzel and dips it so far into the hummus pretty soon all you can see is a glob of hummus and no pretzel at all. "I mean, you know that, right?"

I shrug. "I guess. Kinda. Sorta. Not really."

"And ummmm, not feeling your feelings and pretending things are great even when they're definitely *not* great, is really, really bad. . . ." She pauses and picks a crumb off the crumb cake. "You can't, like, invent a story in your head and then convince yourself it's reality."

I think Mack isn't totally getting this heart-to-heart concept. It's turning more into a lecture, maybe even a TED Talk, but I'll let it go. It's her first one. Gracie and I used to have heart-to-hearts like every day. It was kind of our hobby.

"Yeah, I hear you . . . on all of that." I pause. "How do you know all of this, though?"

"When I'm bored, I download self-help books on the library app on my phone." She pauses. "I'm bored a lot. Obviously. And it hasn't helped me at all. Also obviously. But still."

I laugh. "Wow. Cool. You're very knowledgeable."

"I know." She smiles, seeming all proud.

I lift my eyebrows. "Okay, so yeah . . . Anyway, I kind of just wanted to forget all of that stuff with The Core and Core moms and life in Willets and, yeah."

Mack nods, taking it all in. "Sounds pretty terrible."

I shrug, about to say that there were positives about coming here and my grandparents and all of that. But I stop myself. "It was terrible. Still kind of is." I also want to tell her about the Gracie thing and how she's mad at me, but I'll save that for later. "Also, I know I was kind of a bad friend to you, trying to just smooth over all the bad stuff. Not acknowledging what you were going through . . ."

"See! There you go! You're getting it." She smiles, breaking off a handful of grapes. "Acknowledging when things are hard for people, not creating fake realities, feeling the feelings, baby!" She reaches across the table to high-five me, and it catches me a little off guard. "Feel the feelings! Feelings are okay!"

She's so over the top, kind of screaming about this, so I have to laugh a little. But the truth is, I know she's right. "Okay, so . . . your turn," I say, and unwrap one of Grandpa's dark chocolate squares.

"Well, so, I've always lived here, obviously. My parents are technically married but they hate each other. . . . Anyway, that's not the issue." She laughs and puts her palm to her forehead. "I don't get this, Natty. What am I supposed to do? Just talk about my life?"

I burst into laughter then, too, because it's kind of funny how hard this is for her. "I mean, sure, whatever you want, but I guess I was curious about you and Luna and the rest of that crew, and then Terra and them, also. I don't know. Like what's your deal with friends here?"

"Ooooh." She slow-nods, thinking it over. "I don't have any friends. I was sort of friends with Luna aka Lilian until second grade but then my dad got into a fight with her dad in their bowling league and my dad dropped out and then it was just awkward."

"There's a bowling alley here? I love bowling!"

"Not anymore and it's not like your New York fancy-pants bowling I've seen commercials for. . . . This was like run-down, stale-carpet-smell, old-hot-dogs-in-one-of-those-turny-things bowling."

"That's still fun." I shrug. "I mean, I guess maybe not the old-hot-dogs part? But anyway, go on."

"So that friendship ended, and Terra, Kingsley, and Rowan have always been mean. For as long as I can remember. There used to be a fourth—her name was Valentina—she switched to Catholic school because they turned on her in fifth grade."

"Ouch. Really?"

"Yeah, do you ever hear them say, 'Don't be a Valentina'? That's what they're talking about." She shakes her head. "It's so rude, and they say it wayyyy too much."

"Oh. Yeah, I have heard them say that, actually."

"Yeah. They had been 'KRTV' and they pretended they had a news station and they even had sparkly pink microphones and they'd go around interviewing people . . . like a TV news network . . . get it?"

I nod again. She seems to have a lot to say about this.

"So basically Lilian was my best friend, but then the bowling feud happened and KRTV was so mean to me . . . and for whatever reason, I never made real friends." She pauses. "Until you came. And now Terra is actually nice to me. And I think Lilian, I mean *Luna*, whatever her name is now, has moved on from the bowling thing. . . ."

"Yeah, for sure, I think they like you more than you realize, Mack." I dip another pretzel into the hummus. We're almost finished with it; soon we'll be scraping the sides of the container.

"So that was a heart-to-heart?" she asks. "Did I do it right?"

"You did great, Mack." I smile.

"Thanks. You're coming around, Natty." She pauses. "I'll look online for a new patch for your backpack. It'll say, 'Good Vibes Sometimes.' 'Good Vibes When They Feel Right.' Something along those lines. . . . K?" She thinks for a second. "Maybe even 'Feel Your Feelings'?"

"K." I smile. "Those all sound like good patches."

28

AFTER THREE DAYS AT HOME, it starts to feel like school will never actually open again. The teachers picket outside the elementary, junior high, and high school buildings from eight in the morning until eight at night each day, and the local news covers it, and it's a whole thing.

The teachers in the district are fighting for actual sick days, funding so they won't have to buy their own dry-erase markers anymore, and healthier and more edible food in the cafeteria. Other things, too, I think.

After that one meeting with the parents at school, my dad is home the whole time I'm home. I guess Ms. Lamlot is busy picketing and doesn't have time to hang out with him.

It feels kind of weird to have him around again. Of course, he's not the way he was before. He's dressed and showered and he participates in conversations and he doesn't sleep until two in the afternoon. He's fully back at work, on his laptop in meetings, helping to generate marketing ideas with his colleagues.

Gracie still hasn't called me, and I haven't called her, and the longer we go without speaking, the more awful it seems.

"Natty," Dad says as I'm loading the dishwasher one night after dinner.

"Yeah?" I say, not turning around to face him.

"Can we talk? Can we go for a walk? Or a drive for Dairy Queen?" he asks. "I'm open. I just want to talk to you."

I don't want to agree but the thought of a chocolate Blizzard with Oreos is so appealing I can't resist it. We haven't been to Dairy Queen once since we've been in Miller Creek, and I'm not sure why. It's my favorite.

"Dairy Queen sounds good," I say, but I still don't turn around. I can't bring myself to look at him. I don't know if I'll ever be able to really look at him again.

"Okay, wonderful," he replies, pretty much the most excited I've heard him in a while. "I'll be waiting in the car. Come when you're ready. They do close at nine, though, so I guess be ready before then."

He laughs, but I don't.

I'm not ready to laugh with him yet.

242

I get out to the car a few minutes later and he's sitting there with both seat warmers on, listening to the Rolling Stones song "You Can't Always Get What You Want" and it feels like a scene from a bad movie—so over-the-top obvious—but on the ride over to Dairy Queen we're quiet so I'm forced to listen to the lyrics.

"But if you try sometimes, you get what you need."

Is that true? Sort of, kind of, maybe, I guess.

"Natty, I'm sorry about everything," my dad says, turning the music off.

I pretty much hate when people say they're sorry. It sounds like pity because it is pity and I really don't like pity.

"You don't need to be sorry," I tell him in a soft voice.

"Well, I am. I don't really know how to handle much right now. I guess you've probably realized by now that adults don't always know what they're doing."

I half smile. "Yeah, I've realized that."

He sighs. "I wish I had a way to make sense of everything, Natty, or to tell you it would all be okay, or to even explain what's going on. It's sort of left me frozen somehow. And I'm not sure where we go from here. . . ."

I look over at him as he's driving and I feel like there's so much I could say right now but I don't want to. I want him to come up with some kind of answer, explanation. Something.

"I know it's weird with me and Gwen—I mean, um, Ms.

243

Lamlot, I guess. We're just friends, enjoying each other's company." He pauses. "I still love your mother, Natty, and I miss her, and I want her to be here, and . . ." He sniffles. "I want her to be happy. . . . I don't know."

"Mmmhmm." Suddenly my stomach twists up again and I'm worried I won't even be able to eat the chocolate Oreo Blizzard when we get there.

It's quiet in the car then, no one's saying anything, and I can't take it anymore. "I just wanted to make Mom realize that we could be happy here, that Miller Creek could be a good place to live. I wanted to make the town happier. I wanted to just fix everything," I ramble on, my voice getting louder and louder. "I wanted to pretend everything was fine. Great, even. Because on some level I thought if I did that, everything would be fine, would be great."

"I know, Natty. And it was a valiant effort. Really." He looks over at me when we're at a red light. "But unfortunately it just doesn't always work that way."

"It probably never works that way," I correct him. "I wish someone had told me that, though, before I tried so hard and was going to fail anyway. You could've told me!"

"I'm sorry about that, too. I should have talked to you, really talked to you, a while ago." He sniffles and wipes a tear from the corner of his eye with an old Dunkin' Donuts napkin he has in the cupholder between the seats. "I'm just so sorry."

We get to Dairy Queen and there's only one person there ordering. I remember really long lines here in the summer when I was younger visiting my grandparents, but it's cold now and it's the end of the season and many people disagree with me that ice cream is year-round food.

We order our Blizzards and sit on the low stone wall on the side of the parking lot. It definitely feels freezing eating out here and I need to hold my cup with gloves on but neither of us suggest going to eat in the car.

Somehow, I think the cold feels good. Refreshing, even.

"I miss Mom," I say, sniffling. "I really miss her. I miss her so much it hurts. Like, physically hurts me—in my heart and my head and my stomach. It hurts so much. I don't want to go through the rest of my life without a mom, or I guess with a mom who lives far away."

"I know, Natty. I know. I want us to work something out," he says. "I want things to be good for you."

I look at him then and wait for him to say something else. Something comforting. Or reassuring. But that's it. His thoughts are, like, suspended in midair somehow, and I realize he can't say more because he doesn't have the words and he doesn't even know what to say.

He's lost. My dad is lost. And my mom is lost. And everyone is lost.

I'm lost, too.

But at least I can acknowledge that, now. Admit it. Recognize it. Feel it.

At least I don't need to pretend that everything is great anymore.

I reach my spoon into the bottom of the cup to scoop up the last bits of ice cream. "Okay, we need to get in the car now, though. My fingers are about to fall off."

"Mine, too."

When we get home, I realize that it's early enough that I can still try and catch Gracie before she goes to sleep.

I FaceTime her once and she doesn't answer, but I try again right away, just in case she didn't hear it or something.

"Hi," she says softly after the third ring.

"Hi," I reply. "I'm sorry. I've been a bad friend. I haven't been a good listener. I haven't even been there for you. I'm really, really sorry."

She looks away from the screen. "That is all true."

"Will you talk to me now? Tell me everything," I say. "Please? I promise to listen."

"Okay." She sighs. "I should've seen this coming when everything happened with your mom. The other moms didn't really care, and they talked behind her back, and no one wanted to deal with anything real," Gracie says.

I nod. "Mmmhmm. Go on."

"And, like, our friends aren't really so nice. They're just, like, focused on themselves, and all of a sudden they think I'm *not fun*." She pauses, and tears start trickling down her cheeks. "I didn't change at all! I'm still as fun as I always was, Natty! I don't get it."

My heart hurts, in a way where it feels like it could actually crack in half like the emoji broken heart. "I'm so sorry, Gracie. You're so fun! And I'm sorry I'm not there, and I'm sorry I've been ignoring all of this when you were trying to tell me. I'm sorry I just assumed your life was perfect and would always be perfect, just because it seemed better than mine." I start crying then, too, and soon we're both crying together on FaceTime, and I'm cuddled up under my comforter and I cry and cry and cry.

I finally catch my breath and say, "I miss you, and I miss my mom, and I miss Willets, and I miss the way things used to be. Even if it was fake and turned out bad, I still miss it." I sniffle. "I miss all of it. I miss all of it so much. I never knew it was possible to miss something so much."

"Me, too. I really, really, really do." She grabs a tissue out of the box on her night table. "I don't even know how anything got this way."

"Same. I think that's probably one of the worst parts of the whole thing."

We stay on FaceTime forever, it seems like, so long that soon our eyes get droopy, and we say we're just going to nap together for a little while, but eventually we fully fall asleep. I wake up around three in the morning;

our FaceTime call is still going, but Gracie is completely asleep, snoring away.

I end the call and curl up under my comforter and close my eyes again.

We're all lost. Even Gracie. Mack, too. And we're hurting. I realize that now. On some level, everyone is a little bit lost and a little bit hurting inside.

I'm not going to hide from it anymore. I don't want to hide from it anymore.

THE NIGHT BEFORE WE'RE SUPPOSED to go back to school, Grandma makes baked ziti for dinner. Even though it's one of my favorite meals, I can't really eat it.

"Natty, you okay?" My dad asks, taking another piece of garlic bread off the green platter in the middle of the table.

"Eh, not really." I scoop some food into my mouth. At least if I'm chewing, I can't be expected to talk so much.

Everyone's quiet then, not really asking me any follow-up questions, and they muddle through small-talk conversation about Grandma's card game and how Grandpa's going to be doing some volunteer plumbing work at the senior center.

"It's supposed to reopen next week. Pipes are a mess," he tells us.

He was Miller Creek's most successful plumber for decades and now that he's retired, I bet pipes are probably exploding all over town.

"It'll be good for you to get out there again, Dad," my dad says, and everyone nods, agreeing with him.

"Natty, you having a pep club rehearsal here this evening?" Grandpa asks a minute later, after a sip of his iced tea.

"Huh? No. I have no idea what's going to happen with the pep squad." I pick off a corner of my piece of garlic bread. "I guess we'll see when we get back to school. . . ."

"I'm hearing something outside," Grandpa says, which feels like the strangest thing ever since most of the time he can barely hear us talking from across the table. But then we stay quiet and we all start to hear things. Cheers and shouts and people clapping.

I get up from the table and walk to the dining room window to look outside.

My mouth drops.

They're all standing there, right outside the house, on the front lawn.

Luna, Braid, and Wade.

There are giant letters spelling NATTY made out of duct tape, stretching from one tree to the other, held together by string, and Tape is standing there beside it, looking as proud as I've ever seen her.

Mack is there in her Freddy the Frog costume.

Lance and his friends are there, throwing a little ball to one another like it's a totally normal thing to just have a catch on someone's lawn in the dark.

Terra, Kingsley, and Rowan are there, too. Doing a kick line routine, all bundled up in coats and hats.

"Hey, Pep Squad!" Luna yells.

"Hey!" they all reply.

"Hey, Pep Squad!" Wade takes a turn.

"Hey Hey!"

"Oh my goodness!" I say, running outside, my heart leaping out of my chest, pretty much. "What's happening here?"

Mack keeps jumping up and down in the Freddy the Frog costume, clapping her floppy frog hands.

"We're peppy!" she yells.

And then they all join in with her. "We're peppy! We're peppy! We're the peppiest!"

I guess it's a cheer they made up on their own before they got here, or maybe they're making it up right now on the spot.

"Go, Miller! Go, Creek! Go Go, Miller Creek!" Kingsley and Rowan sing, bouncing up and down, clapping.

"Go, Frogs! Dance around! Go, Frogs!" everyone else yells in response.

"Take it away, Freddy!" Braid shouts.

And then Mack really shows a side of her I've truly never, ever, ever seen before.

She starts bouncing around and dancing, linking arms with all of the other pep squad members.

"Freddy the Frog will show you the way!" she yells, making up a song. "Freddy the Frog FOREVER!"

"Forever!" they say, echoing.

"Go, Freddy! Go, Freddy! Go, Freddy!" They all keep cheering and she dances and bops up and down and everyone dances around her and claps.

They go on doing all of this for another five minutes and I watch and clap and dance a little, too, and finally they're all out of breath, and they take a break. Mack takes off her Freddy the Frog head, brushes the sweat off her forehead with the back of her hand, and smiles at me.

"Natty, we're sorry," Luna says.

"For what? None of what happened was your fault. You didn't go on strike!" I laugh. "You showed up for a pep squad you didn't really even want to be in . . . so. . . ."

"But we want to now," Rowan and Kingsley say in unison, and then start laughing.

Rowan continues, "And we're sad the pep rally didn't happen. And we wanted to, like, have a pep rally right here, right now."

"Honestly, I want the pep squad to succeed," Wade says. "I want to be part of it, too. It's unusual, but that's an element of what makes it great."

"I don't think that's the only thing that makes it great," Braid scoffs.

"I'm here tonight 'cuz they dragged me," Tape admits. "But yeah, whatever, it's cool. I want to make posters totally out of duct tape if that's a possibility. . . . Not sure why I didn't think of it earlier."

"Cool idea, Tape." I smile and look over at Mack. "You still want to be our mascot?"

"Well, yeah. I'm here in a giant frog costume. Would that be happening if I didn't want to?"

"Probably not." I shrug.

"We're here for it, too, man," Lance says, shaking his head. "Here to see whatever happens, because I found a whole new side of myself when I came up with that 'Sweet Caroline' routine. . . ."

"Oh, here we go," Marcus mutters, shaking his head.

"He found a whole new side of himself when he met Natty," Chris says under his breath, doing that fake-cough thing people do. And when he realizes the others and I heard it, he says, "Uhhh, I mean. Never mind."

"Oh my god, Natty!" Mack screams, interrupting the awkwardness. "I have the best idea." She looks out at the group. "Anyone have time for a quick bonfire? We need to have, like, an official Miller Creek Pep Squad bonding experience."

"Say what?" Wade asks.

"I'm way in," Trey says. "I love bonfires."

"Natty, you have a firepit, right?" Mack asks. "Oh! And your grandma makes that s'mores pie, right? Do you still have ingredients?"

"Wow, good memory, Mack," I say. "We do have a firepit, but we haven't used it since I've been here. . . . It may be covered in sticks and leaves and stuff. . . ."

"No problem! We'll clean it off!" Mack is the most excited I've ever seen her and I need to see where this is going. "Let's do it!"

"Uh, don't we need to ask like Natty's dad's permission or something?" Tape asks, eyebrows crinkly in the middle. "Also, I kind of said I'd be home by nine at the latest, so . . ."

"Whoa, now Tape is suddenly a rule follower!" Braid yells. "Everyone's changing so fast."

We all crack up, and then I run inside. Dad and Grandpa have finished eating and Grandma's starting to clean up around my plate.

"Sorry about missing most of dinner, Grandma," I say, looking through the pantry for the s'mores ingredients. "Also, would it be okay if we lit a teeny, tiny fire in the firepit?"

"What?" she gasps. "Clark, please help them. I don't know what's happening."

"Huh?" Grandpa looks up from the dish rack, where he's drying a glass.

I explain that we're having a quick bonfire and he reluctantly agrees to help, getting out the long lighter and some old newspapers.

When I get back outside, everyone has already pulled chairs over to be in a little circle around the firepit. They're all talking and laughing, and I quickly take my phone out of my pocket to snap a picture.

"Okay, I have all the s'mores ingredients, and my grandpa's gonna help us light the fire," I explain.

"Make this quick, please," Grandpa says, pulling his hat down farther over his ears. "It's frigid out here!"

"I have gathered the sticks," Lance says in a weird official-sounding tone, trying to sound old-fashioned or something. I'm not sure what, but it's funny and I crack up.

Terra shakes her head at me and smiles.

We sit around for a while and roast marshmallows and make s'mores and chat and laugh.

"I should've brought my guitar," Wade says.

"You play guitar?" I ask, shocked.

"He does." Braid smiles, sitting back, seeming sort of proud. "Wait, can we burn stuff right now? Like in a cleansing kind of way. I have this note in my jacket pocket that I had to get signed about how I failed my math test."

"Sure! Go ahead. Burn away." I laugh.

"Ooh, I love to burn stuff," Kingsley adds. "I should've brought all those love notes John Kellerson wrote me last year . . . before he RUINED MY LIFE."

"Okay, calm down, Kingsie, whoa." Rowan puts a hand on her shoulder. "Mega intensity right now."

I jump in to say, "See? The old me would have said *everything happens for a reason* and *look how resilient you are to overcome it* . . . about whatever happened with John."

"OMG! That's EXACTLY what we need to burn!" Mack screams, and it's kind of amazing how much more comfortable she feels around everyone now. "Toxic positivity!"

"What?" Tape asks.

"Like toxic positive phrases, basically all the over-the-top stuff Natty says." She jabs me with her elbow in a playful way. "JK."

I shake my head. "Nah, it's okay. It's kinda true."

Mack continues, "Natty has come such a long way and she realizes now that she doesn't need to be positive allll the time and she can actually FEEL HER FEELINGS!" she shouts. "Let's write toxic positive phrases like 'good vibes only' on a piece of paper and burn them all in the firepit. Come on! WE NEED TO DO THIS, PEOPLE!"

"I don't know this girl, but she's pretty cool," I hear Chris whisper to Lance.

Tape says, "I don't have paper, but I do have duct tape. . . . Should we use that?"

"No," I jump in. "Burning that feels like, actually toxic, somehow." I laugh. "I mean, no pun intended but for real."

Everyone laughs at that and I get an all-over proud, jazz-hands kind of feeling that I could make them laugh and that we're all having fun hanging out together.

"I'll go in and get paper and pens."

I run back inside and Dad, Grandma, and Grandpa are sitting around the table, drinking tea, smiling, and seeming relaxed and content. I grab some little pads of paper from Grandma's junk drawer and whatever pens are in there and head back outside.

"Having fun, Natty?" my dad asks.

I nod. "Yup. Gotta get back out there."

He nods. "Enjoy."

I'm back outside, handing out the paper and pens, and I look up and see a zillion stars. And even though it's freezing, there's something so great about this moment: a bonfire with friends in my new town, all bundled up in coats and hats and gloves.

I'm not just saying it's great because I want it to be great. It actually is great.

"Okay, everyone, write quick, because it's too cold to have our gloves off," Mack says. "Go, go, go!"

"Can I just say I still have zero clue what we're doing?" Kingsley says.

"Um, same. Literally no clue," Rowan adds.

"Just write down a phrase that people say to try and be helpful that isn't at all and totally makes the person feel worse like, 'The Universe never gives you more than you can handle' and stuff . . . ," Mack says. "Like, 'Just think positive!' 'Look on the bright side.' 'Attitude is Everything.' Blah blah blah."

"Ah, okay!" Terra says. "I get it now. Natty does say that stuff *a lot*."

Everyone writes down their phrases and we throw them all in the fire, and none of us say what we write down, but we all stand there, gathered around the firepit, watching the flames.

"This was fun," Braid says, and then looks at me. "And I know we give you a hard time and you're kind of annoying. But we also, kind of . . ." She glances around at everyone else. "We kind of actually like you, I think. And not just 'cuz you bring us lunch . . ."

"Dude, what? You bring them lunch?" Lance asks, shocked.

The rest of them nod.

I smile. "Well, cool. I kind of actually like you all, too."

We stand there talking for a few more minutes and then we walk back around to the front yard. Everyone yells "thank you for the lunches" to Grandma inside the house before they leave.

Mack stays for a little longer, and she sits down on my front steps holding the frog head. I sit next to her.

"You okay, Natty?" she asks.

"Yeah. I'm great," I say, sitting down next to her. "Okay, no, I'll start again. I'm actually not great. I mean, I'm sad and confused and overwhelmed and hungry since I didn't finish my dinner . . . and so many other feelings all smooshed in there, that I'm basically a rainbow-tie-dyed jumpsuit of emotion, but yeah, I'm great, too."

"That sounds very cool, actually. I'd wear that." She smiles.

I laugh. "You would?"

"Yeah, totally. Let's get matching ones."

"Done." I smile.

Mack leans over and rests her head on my shoulder, and even though it's freezing out, we stay that way for a while.

"No, but for real, Natty, you sure you're okay?" she asks again.

"Absolutely, positively."

And for the first time, in a long, long, long time, it's actually the truth.

Acknowledgments

Thank you, thank you, thank you to Aleah, my darling daughter and unofficial editor, who reads my books and gives me phenomenal constructive criticism.

To Hazel, my darling daughter and snuggling champion, thank you for all the cuddles, hugs, and parking suggestions.

Dave, thank you for loving me and believing in me and for listening to me ask the same questions over and over again, especially when you don't have the answers.

Kibbitz, you are a dream dog, and I cannot imagine life without you.

Maria, you are a guiding force of infinite wisdom and I am so grateful for your gentle touch and insightful feedback.

Sara, thank you for all of your phenomenal notes and feedback. You are brilliant!

Katherine Tegen and the entire team—Jon, Gweneth, Kristen, Molly, Amy, Anna, and Vaishali: thank you for all the hard work and love you put into my books. I am forever grateful.

Alexandra, thanks for the great cover art!

David, Lauren, Max, Shana, Bobbi, and Joseph: thank you for caring about me, supporting me, and showing interest in my books.

Rosenberg Crew, there are so many of you: thanks for the encouragement and for asking about my books and my writing.

Caroline Hickey, Lisa Graff, Goldy Moldavsky: you are rock-star writers and rock-star pals and I wouldn't be able to make it on this creative journey without you.

Finally, to anyone reading this: I wish you the ability to feel your feelings and for people to love you, support you, and acknowledge your struggles, your losses, and your heartaches.

Great books by LISA GREENWALD!

The Friendship List

TBH

KATHERINE TEGEN BOOKS
An Imprint of HarperCollins Publishers

harpercollinschildrens.com